No More Kidding Around . . .

A pistol barked to Longarm's left, one slug tearing into the floor near Longarm's left knee, the other drilling a table leg and throwing splinters in all directions. The lawman turned to see that Kid McQuade had finally gotten his pants up and had grabbed a hogleg. He was triggering the pearl-gripped Remington as he sidestepped toward the bar, about fifteen feet away from Longarm, and screaming, his mouth and eyes wide.

The lawman rolled beneath a table. Two slugs chewed through the table and into the floor.

Longarm rolled out from under the table and triggered both his Colt and his derringer. The Colt's .44 round hammered the kid's forehead above his left eye while the derringer's .32-caliber slug drilled a neat, marble-sized hole through his right cheek, just beneath the same eye.

The kid took one more side step toward the bar, nodding his head sharply as though he agreed with something that had been said, then stopped and dropped straight down to his knees. He nodded once more, thick curly hair bouncing about his neck and shoulders, then flopped onto his back, arms spread out to both sides and flapping like wings. His spurred boots clicked madly on the wooden floor . . .

DON'T MISS THESE
ALL-ACTION WESTERN SERIES
FROM THE BERKLEY PUBLISHING GROUP

THE GUNSMITH by J. R. Roberts

Clint Adams was a legend among lawmen, outlaws, and ladies. They called him . . . the Gunsmith.

LONGARM by Tabor Evans

The popular long-running series about Deputy U.S. Marshal Custis Long—his life, his loves, his fight for justice.

SLOCUM by Jake Logan

Today's longest-running action Western. John Slocum rides a deadly trail of hot blood and cold steel.

BUSHWHACKERS by B. J. Lanagan

An action-packed series by the creators of Longarm! The rousing adventures of the most brutal gang of cutthroats ever assembled—Quantrill's Raiders.

DIAMONDBACK by Guy Brewer

Dex Yancey is Diamondback, a Southern gentleman turned con man when his brother cheats him out of the family fortune. Ladies love him. Gamblers hate him. But nobody pulls one over on Dex . . .

WILDGUN by Jack Hanson

The blazing adventures of mountain man Will Barlow—from the creators of Longarm!

TEXAS TRACKER by Tom Calhoun

J.T. Law: the most relentless—and dangerous—manhunter in all Texas. Where sheriffs and posses fail, he's the best man to bring in the most vicious outlaws—for a price.

TABOR EVANS

LONGARM

AND THE SINS
OF LAUGHING LYLE

J

JOVE BOOKS, NEW YORK

THE BERKLEY PUBLISHING GROUP
Published by the Penguin Group
Penguin Group (USA) Inc.
375 Hudson Street, New York, New York 10014, USA

Penguin Group (Canada), 90 Eglinton Avenue East, Suite 700, Toronto, Ontario M4P 2Y3, Canada (a division of Pearson Penguin Canada Inc.) • Penguin Books Ltd., 80 Strand, London WC2R 0RL, England • Penguin Group Ireland, 25 St. Stephen's Green, Dublin 2, Ireland (a division of Penguin Books Ltd.) • Penguin Group (Australia), 250 Camberwell Road, Camberwell, Victoria 3124, Australia (a division of Pearson Australia Group Pty. Ltd.) • Penguin Books India Pvt. Ltd., 11 Community Centre, Panchsheel Park, New Delhi—110 017, India • Penguin Group (NZ), 67 Apollo Drive, Rosedale, Auckland 0632, New Zealand (a division of Pearson New Zealand Ltd.) • Penguin Books (South Africa) (Pty.) Ltd., 24 Sturdee Avenue, Rosebank, Johannesburg 2196, South Africa

Penguin Books Ltd., Registered Offices: 80 Strand, London WC2R 0RL, England

This is a work of fiction. Names, characters, places, and incidents either are the product of the author's imagination or are used fictitiously, and any resemblance to actual persons, living or dead, business establishments, events, or locales is entirely coincidental.

LONGARM AND THE SINS OF LAUGHING LYLE

A Jove Book / published by arrangement with the author

PUBLISHING HISTORY
Jove edition / November 2012

Copyright © 2012 by Penguin Group (USA) Inc.
Cover illustration by Milo Sinovcic.

ISBN: 978-0-515-15118-3

JOVE®
Jove Books are published by The Berkley Publishing Group, a division of Penguin Group (USA) Inc., 375 Hudson Street, New York, New York 10014. JOVE® is a registered trademark of Penguin Group (USA) Inc. The "J" design is a trademark of Penguin Group (USA) Inc.

PRINTED IN THE UNITED STATES OF AMERICA

10 9 8 7 6 5 4 3 2 1

ALWAYS LEARNING   **PEARSON**

Chapter 1

"Lyle May—well, I'll be damned," said Deputy U.S. Marshal Case Morgan, a gob of blood oozing out between his lips to dribble down his spade-bearded chin. "We finally got him."

"Easy, Case," said Morgan's colleague, Custis P. Long, the lawman known far and wide as Longarm. "You rest easy." He leaned his rifle down against a boulder and pulled his canteen off his saddle horn. He crouched beside the other lawman, about ten years Longarm's senior, and held his canteen out to him.

Morgan wrapped a gloved hand around the flask, drew it to his lips. As he drank, Longarm looked at the bloody bandage down low on the man's right side, just above his double cartridge belts. The bandage was soaked and glistening. The wound had opened again. Not good, Longarm thought. Not good at all. Morgan needed a saw-bones bad.

"Never mind about that."

Longarm lifted his gaze to Case's blue eyes regarding him shrewdly, a smile twitching at the older lawman's mustache-mantled mouth. "I'll be fine, Custis. You go in and drag them killers out here kickin' and screamin'. I wanna see 'em. Especially Laughing Lyle. After what he did in Stoneville . . ." Case shook his head. "I wanna see the look in that yellow-toothed demon's eyes when you throw the cuffs on him."

"All right, Case." Longarm squeezed the man's arm, reluctant to leave his friend out here in the brush and rocks. He'd been spitting up blood for several hours. That meant the bullet had done somethin' bad to his insides. Very bad . . .

"Then we'll get me tended," Case said reassuringly. "But first things first."

"All right."

Longarm glanced at the bloody wound again, saw the gauntness of Morgan's withered cheeks, the red in the whites of his eyes. He should have gotten Morgan over to Albuquerque right after May's men bushwhacked them and drilled that slug into Morgan's side. But Case had insisted they continue following May while his trail was still warm.

The bushwhacking had been three days ago. Three days' worth of blood loss for Case Morgan. Those three days might have punched the older lawman's ticket, and the thought wrenched Longarm's own insides as he set the canteen down beside his friend and stood.

"All right, Case," he said. "As soon as I clear the rats out of that little hellhole yonder, we'll get you in there, find you a bed, get you a shot of whiskey, maybe a bowl of chili."

"How 'bout a whore? I sure could use a poke, Custis."

"You got it. A whore, to boot!"

Morgan chuckled beneath the brim of his broad-brimmed, tan hat as he sat there against the rock, one long leg clad in dusty corduroy poking straight out in front of him, the other curled inward so that his high-topped boot touched the calf of the other leg. Morgan's chest rose and fell slowly, shallowly, behind his collarless, blue pin-striped shirt and the brown leather vest to which his deputy marshal's badge was pinned.

"Sorry, Custis." The older lawman narrowed a sheepish eye at Longarm, who picked up his rifle and rubbed dust from the receiver before working the cocking mechanism and racking a shell into the chamber. "I led us right into that bushwhack. Damn, I must be gettin' too old for this shit."

"Shut up, Case. May's a sneaky devil."

"I scouted that trail, so I shoulda known. A few years ago I *would have* known. Instead, I led us both right into that nest of rifles." Morgan punched the ground beside him, causing a feather of tan dust to rise and catch the weakening, wheat-colored rays of the late-day New Mexico sun.

"We both rode into them rifles together, hoss. Now, shut up and get some sleep." Longarm grabbed the reins of the dusty gray he'd rented at a little unnamed outpost on the Arkansas River and slid his rifle into its saddle boot. "I'll be back shortly."

"I know you will, Custis."

Longarm swung into the saddle, not wanting to think about what would happen to his partner if he didn't return. He glanced once more at the older lawman slumped against the boulder, and turned the gray around and headed back south through the brush and piñon pines.

The roadhouse where Laughing Lyle May and his three partners, Richard Dix, Kid McQuade, and Charlie Embers were holed up lay to the north. Longarm and Morgan had ridden in from the south. He'd decided after scouting the roadhouse earlier on foot that he'd head back to the stage trail and follow it into the yard, like any other traveler would do, so as not to draw suspicion. Judging by the leisurely way the gang had been riding for the past two days, they no longer thought anyone was trailing them.

And, since Longarm didn't think they'd gotten a good look at him back where they'd ambushed him and Case Morgan, there was no point in skulking around the roadhouse, waiting for the four to come out. That might not happen until morning, and he needed to get Case into a bed with food and whiskey in his belly.

He'd walk into the place casual-like and try to take the four by surprise. Faster, that way. As long as they really hadn't seen him and didn't drill him as he stepped across the threshold . . .

He swung back to the stage road and headed north. A couple minutes later, the roadhouse appeared at the base of a sandstone ridge, a corral and privy flanking it. It was a broad adobe affair, weathered by time and the desert sands, and it sported a tall wooden façade that announced WILBUR FINLAY'S.

When Longarm had scouted the place before, tramping around behind it and peering in a window, the killers and bank robbers he was stalking were playing slap and tickle with a couple of whores at a table near the bar. Besides a beefy half-breed barman, there'd been three other men inside, area cowpunchers most likely, bellying up to the bar. Their three horses were still tethered to the hitch rack to the left of the broad, stone steps, belly straps and bits hanging free.

Keeping an eye on the windows and the two front doors closed behind the batwings—it was cool at this altitude this late in the day, and a nasty wind had been blowing off and on—Longarm put the gray up to the hitch rack. He swung down from the saddle, looped the reins over the smoothly worn pine-pole crossbar, and considered sliding his Winchester from its saddle scabbard.

Deciding the long gun would invite suspicion and possibly cause things to pop prematurely, Longarm left the rifle in its boot. His double-action Frontier Colt .44 in the cross-draw holster on his left hip, and the over-and-under derringer snugged in his vest pocket, under the right flap of his brown frock coat, would have to suffice.

Eight bullets for four men should be four bullets too many.

He adjusted his snuff-brown, low-crowned, flat-brimmed Stetson and brushed dust from his brown tweed trousers stuffed into the tops of his mule-eared, low-heeled cavalry boots. Longarm was a big man, face bronzed by the frontier sun, shoulders broad, long legs dropping from a narrow waist. A longhorn mustache mantled his wide mouth, under brown eyes set deep in bony sockets. He opened the double doors and stepped into Finlay's, quickly closing the doors behind him, then turning to face the room, shaping a disarming grin and wagging his head. "Whew! Wind's pickin' up again. Gonna be a cold night, I'm afeared!"

"Sure is, mister. Come on in and get yourself warmed up." This from the beefy bartender—a thick man with long, dark brown hair and heavy pouches under his eyes.

As before, three punchers stood at the bar, now with heads turned toward the newcomer, each with a boot hooked atop the brass foot rail. However, there were only two outlaws at the table that all four had been sitting at a half hour ago. One was stomping drunkenly up the wooden stairs at the back of the room, an arm wrapped around a whore in a pink Bordeaux corset with black neck stockings, garters, and black, high-heeled shoes. She was giggling and clutching the stair rail while her bald, broad-backed jake in a pinto vest and red-and-white striped trousers staggered and swung a bottle around with his free hand, yelling and laughing raucously.

That would be Laughing Lyle.

Two of the three other cutthroats sat at their table playing cards inside a thickly billowing cloud of tobacco smoke. A third was fucking another whore on a fainting couch near a woodstove against the room's left-side wall, behind them. This third man had his pants and red long handles down around his ankles, and he hammered away between the whore's spread legs, grunting loudly with each violent thrust. The groaning whore, legs flapping like wings, was completely naked save for the purple feathers adorning her hair. Her clothes, few as there were, lay about the floor near the couch, a pair of pink panties and a garter belt hanging from the elk horn on the wall above her and the man she was entertaining.

No one else in the saloon was paying attention to the lovers. All eyes were on Longarm, who grinned with feigned sheepishness and ran a hand across his mustache as he strolled casually toward the bar. "Well, looks like somone's havin' fun, anyways. Good night for it. I reckon we all oughta be buddyin' up."

"I got a couple more upstairs," the half-breed said. "They don't go on duty for another hour, though. I'd wake 'em up if you offered to pay double, but they're in better moods if you let 'em have their full beauty rest. You know women."

"Purely I do. And that's all right," Longarm said, noticing that the two cutthroats playing poker at the table behind him were eyeing him in the backbar mirror. "I reckon just a whiskey to cut the dust'll do me."

The other three men, dressed in the grubby trail garb of thirty-a-month-and-found trail hands, had gone back to their own private conversation, the one in the middle putting his back to the bar so he could speak to the men on either side of him. The cutthroat fucking the whore was still grunting and causing the legs of the fainting couch to squawk against the worn floor puncheons.

"Oh Jesus, oh God," the whore was saying, obviously bored.

When Longarm ordered a shot of whiskey, the barman popped the cork on a bottle and glanced at the pair on the far side of the room before returning his gaze to his newest customer. "Said he couldn't wait long enough to get upstairs," the barman said, meaning the cutthroat fucking the whore. "My guess is he's too *drunk* to climb the stairs. Been goin' at it for ten minutes, now."

"Sure does make a fuss about it," Longarm said, sipping the whiskey and keeping an eye on the two cutthroats who in turn were keeping an eye on him as they flipped their pasteboards around. He sipped his drink and wondered how he was going to play his own hand.

He had two in one spot, another on the fainting couch, and Laughing Lyle upstairs. Longarm could still hear Lyle laughing up there, though the laughter was muffled by the ceiling. More than only his laughter had pegged him. May was built like a rain barrel, bald on the top of his head but with long, stringy blond hair falling down the sides and the back. He had a face like a bulldog.

A mean one.

A rabid one with a taste for human flesh.

The killer on the left side of the table was likely Richard Dix, with the telltale rope burn across his throat and the Buntline Special in a shoulder holster. Sitting on the left side of the table was Charlie Embers—black-haired and black-mustached, with the black, mean eyes to go with his reputation of being as agreeable as a caged rattlesnake. He had two Smith & Wesson pistols on the table before him, and he kept glancing Longarm's way and giving one of the pistols a menacing little spin.

Since Longarm had identified Laughing Lyle, Dix, and Embers, the man on the fainting couch was likely Kid McQuade, though Longarm couldn't see much of the Kid back in the shadows except his floury-white ass bouncing up and down between the whore's flopping knees.

"Hey, *you!*" one of the cutthroats shouted behind Longarm. In the back-bar mirror, he saw Charlie Embers shove his chair back and rise a little unsteadily, his mean, dark eyes riveted on Longarm's in the mirror. "Yeah, *you*—what in *holy hell* you starin' at, mister?"

He tossed his cards down, grabbed his pistol off the table, and started stomping angrily toward Longarm.

Chapter 2

Longarm gave an inward groan as he turned toward Charlie Embers swaggering toward him heavy-footed and bleary-eyed but managing to twirl his pistols rather adeptly, with obvious threat.

The lawman tried hard to keep his affable grin in place. It wasn't easy, knowing what these men had done to Case Morgan, not to mention the bank they'd robbed in Stoneville, in western Kansas, then setting the place afire with all the employees and patrons locked inside.

Laughing Lyle May's bunch had killed several more citizens and a sheriff's deputy as they'd stormed out of town with sixteen thousand dollars in stolen greenbacks, shooting at anything that moved, Laughing Lyle looking like a moon-crazed hyena. Killing the lawman and crossing state lines was what had made their latest dastardly deed, only one of many, the business of the federal marshals. That's why Chief Marshal Billy Vail had assigned Longarm to throw in with Case Morgan out of Fort Smith, Arkansas, to try and run the small, deadly gang to ground. Longarm had worked with Case Morgan many times over his long career; he'd come to revere the man like few others, so he was gritting his teeth behind his smile as Charlie Embers stepped up to within one foot of him . . .

So close that Longarm's nostrils twitched at the nastiness of the man's rancid smell, as though it emanated from deep within his rotten, kill-crazy soul. Embers smelled like an ear preserved in rotgut whiskey.

"Why you find us so damned fascinatin'?" Charlie said.

"Ah, hell, mister, I didn't mean to be snoopy and get your neck in a hump," Longarm said, manufacturing a faintly wheedling, cowardly tone, holding his hands up to his shoulders in supplication. "I was just wonderin' what kind of a game you got goin' and if maybe another man could sit in—that's all."

Embers's head only came up to Longarm's chin, so the killer had to look up at the lawman from beneath his shaggy, black brows, while holding his pistols about six inches from Longarm's belly. He was faintly walleyed from drink. "Oh, you did, didja, Mister Francy-Dresser?"

Charlie cast his angry gaze across Longarm's fawn vest, worn over a blue cotton shirt down which a black string tie dangled. Working his nostrils like a gut-sniffing dog, he looked once more into Longarm's eyes from beneath his black, shaggy brows. "Well, suppose me and my pal don't want no fancy-dressin' cardsharp sittin' in on our game. Supposin' we don't play with sharpies?"

Longarm shrugged. "Well, okay, then. I don't see no reason to get your neck up about it."

"We work hard for our money, see. That's why I get my neck up about it."

The man at the table, Richard Dix, chuckled at that as he stared toward Embers and Longarm. Behind him, Kid McQuade had finally attained full pleasure with the whore and was sitting back, breathing hard with his pants still down around his ankles, knees spread, while the whore remained on her back, groaning miserably and cupping her hands to her snatch. She was plumb worn out, it seemed.

"I'm sure you do work hard for it," Longarm told Charlie. "And I do apologize if you for some reason got to believin' I'd think otherwise!"

"I could just shoot you—you know that," Charlie said, gritting his teeth and ramming his pistol barrels against Longarm's belly. "I really could. I could just shoot a damn worthless cardsharp that don't know how to make his livin' no other way than sittin' around poker tables and roulette wheels. I'll be damned if you just don't make me madder'n an old wet hen, sir!"

Longarm saw in Charlie's sparking eyes that the killer's wolf was indeed off its leash. Charlie hadn't killed in a couple of days, and the lack of fresh blood on his hands, coupled with the whiskey he'd been drinking for the past several hours, was making him ornery.

Apprehension made the lawman's shoulders tighten as he stared down at the cocked pistols the insane killer held taut against his fawn-colored vest, over the gold-washed chain that connected Longarm's railroad watch in one pocket to his derringer in the other.

Wouldn't it just be funny if he'd outsmarted himself here and got himself killed because the gang thought he was a professional poker player? Certainly not to Case Morgan, who was bleeding dry out in the stony hollow yonder.

Longarm slid his gaze back up to Charlie's. The lawman felt a slight shudder of rage sweep through him, and he tightened his jaws against it. The three punchers had fallen silent and were staring apprehensively toward Charlie and Longarm. In fact, all eyes in the room were on the pair—even those of the whore as she lay on her side on the fainting couch beside the grinning Kid McQuade, who still hadn't bothered to pull his pants up.

"Oh, you don't like that—do you?" Charlie said, ramming the pistol barrels harder against Longarm's belly and grinning with mockery. "You might be a big nancyboy poker player, but you're gettin' mad. You don't like bein' pushed, do ya?" Charlie turned to the man at the poker table and laughed. "Hey, Richard—I'm makin' Mister Fancy Dresser *mad!*"

Charlie tensed suddenly. Keeping his head turned toward Dix, he rolled one eye down toward the over-and-under peashooter that Longarm was now holding taut against Charlie's lower jaw, on the right side of Charlie's face. Longarm drew the derringer's hammer back with a ratcheting click that sounded inordinately loud now in the heavy silence.

"You got that right, Charlie," Longarm said with menacing softness. "You've done made me mad."

At the poker table, Richard Dix's smile faded, and the card-playing killer stiffened in his chair. Behind him, Kid McQuade, who probably couldn't see Charlie and Longarm clearly from the far side of the room, merely wrinkled his brows.

Charlie grunted. He showed chipped, yellow teeth beneath his black mustache as he winced against the pressure of Longarm's gold-chased peashooter.

"So mad, in fact, Charlie," Longarm continued evenly, "that if you don't uncock those hoglegs and remove them from my midsection, I'm going to blow a hole through your ugly fuckin' head."

Instantly, the mocking anger in Charlie's eyes turned to fear and befuddlement. He drew the pistols back from Longarm's belly but kept them aimed and cocked as he said, "H-how do you know my name?"

"How do you think, you cow-stupid fucker?" Longarm paused. "Lower the hammers easy-like, Charlie, or we'll die together . . . do us a little dance while we're fallin' to the floor and lassoin' the next cloud to Glory!"

Richard Dix bounded to his feet so quickly that his chair tumbled to the floor with a raucous clatter. "Hey, what the *shit!*"

"Keep still, Richard," Charlie said in a quavering, high-pitched voice as he stared sidelong at Longarm's derringer boring a white dent in his cheek. "The man's mad an' he's holdin' a gun to my gall-blasted jaw!"

He depressed the hammers of his two pistols.

"Go ahead and drop 'em on the floor, Charlie," Longarm said.

"Ah, *hell!*" Charlie said, and threw the pistols onto the floor, one on either side of him and Longarm.

The three cowpunchers had moved on down the bar and were tightly bunched, watching the unfriendly proceedings uneasily. They'd come to Finlay's for a quiet drink out of the wind—and now this?

As Longarm walked Charlie back toward his table,

where Dix stood scowling, one hand wrapped around the butt of the Buntline Special riding in his shoulder holster, the whore laughed delightedly from the fainting couch.

"Shit!" said Kid McQuade, standing awkwardly, then stumbling forward over his trousers and balbriggans, and hitting the floor on his knees. He looked up at Longarm, shaking a curly mop of brown hair out of his eyes. "You best holster that weapon, mister. You don't know who we are!"

Longarm gave Charlie one more hard shove with his derringer. Charlie gave an agonized cry and stumbled into his table. Longarm then flipped his derringer in the air. He caught it in his left hand while reaching across his flat belly with his right and sliding the Frontier Colt . 44 from the cross-draw holster on his left hip.

He leveled both weapons on the cutthroats. "I know who you are," Longarm said, glancing past the three waddies on his right toward the stairs, uneasy about Laughing Lyle May, whom he could no longer hear laughing. "I'm Custis Long, deputy U.S. marshal out of Denver, and you fellas done come to the end of your trail."

"Don't think so, Long!" came the roaring shout from the stairs.

Longarm swung to his right. As though he'd materialized out of thin air, Laughing Lyle stood a third of the way down the stairs, gritting his teeth and leveling two Colts.

"*Down, boys!*" Longarm shouted at the drovers, diving straight forward, away from the table, just as Laughing Lyle opened up with his Colts, sending lead screaming around the saloon hall and chewing into the floor behind Longarm's boots.

The three waddies hurled themselves, chaps flapping, up and over the bar, to hit the floor on the other side with heavy slapping thuds. Laughing Lyle cut loose with a tooth-gnashing yell as he continued triggering his six-guns. At the same time, Longarm hit the floor to the left of Dix and Charlie Embers, and Laughing Lyle shouted at his two cohorts, "Get outta the way, you stupid bastards, or I'll turn you both into stew!"

Longarm rolled and came up on his butt, extending his Colt and derringer as Laughing Lyle triggered a round into the table about four feet ahead of the lawman, blowing up splinters and playing cards between Dix and Charlie Embers. Longarm fired twice quickly at Laughing Lyle, hammering adobe out of the wall behind him and causing the outlaw to wheel drunkenly and fall to the stairs.

Meanwhile, Dix had fallen atop a chair but was scrambling back to his feet red-faced and pulling the long-barreled hogleg out of its shoulder holster. Before he could level the big popper, Longarm drilled him with his derringer, the .32-caliber slug taking the tall, lanky killer through his prominent Adam's apple. The slug ricocheted off his spine, exited the left side of his neck, and screamed into the wall over the naked whore cowering with her arms over her head on the fainting couch.

Dix threw his head back and tried to scream, but nothing came out except a shrill choking noise, as he triggered the Buntline Special into the ceiling before he fell and expired. Longarm fired two more shots at Laughing Lyle on the stairs, and then, as Charlie Embers scooped his two pistols off the floor, Longarm shot the black-haired, poison-mean owlhoot twice in the chest.

The slugs picked Charlie straight up off the floor and threw him up and over the bar, behind which he disappeared with a smacking *bang,* evoking indignant cries from the waddies.

A pistol barked to Longarm's left, one slug tearing into the floor near his left knee, the other drilling a table leg and throwing splinters in all directions. The lawman turned to see that Kid McQuade had finally gotten his pants up and grabbed a hogleg. He was triggering the pearl-gripped Remington as he sidestepped toward the bar, about fifteen feet away from Longarm, and screaming, his mouth and eyes wide.

The lawman rolled beneath a table. Two slugs chewed through the table and into the floor.

Longarm rolled out from under the table and triggered both his Colt and his derringer. The Colt's .44 round hammered the kid's forehead above his left eye, while the derringer's .32-caliber slug drilled a neat, marble-sized hole through his left cheek, just beneath the same eye.

The kid took one more side step toward the bar, nodding his head sharply as though he couldn't agree more with something that had been said, then stopped and dropped straight down to his knees. He nodded once more, thick curly hair bouncing about his neck and shoulders, then flopped onto his back, arms spread out to both sides and flapping like wings. His spurred boots clicked madly on the wooden floor.

Suddenly, that was the only sound. It died quickly, and the Kid lay still.

Longarm looked around. The half-breed barman, Charlie Embers, and the three innocent waddies were out of sight behind the bar. Longarm could see only the Kid and Dix, both dead, and the whore, who lay slumped forward over her knees, head beneath her arms, her pale naked rump pointing at the ceiling.

Longarm looked at the stairs. Laughing Lyle was gone.

"Everyone stay down!" Longarm yelled as he stuffed his empty derringer into his vest pocket, then quickly knocked the spent loads out of his Colt's wheel. The smoking brass casings clinked onto the floor and rolled.

Quickly, he reloaded the pistol from his shell belt and ran to the stairs.

Chapter 3

Longarm took the stairs three steps at a time and hurled himself onto the floor of the second-story hall. There were three doors on each side. At the end was a dirty window through which the gray light of dusk pushed through a torn red curtain.

Longarm shifted his gaze from one side of the hall to the other, from one closed door to the next. There appeared no way out of the second story save the stairs behind him. Laughing Lyle had to be up here somewhere, behind one of the six doors.

Longarm pushed slowly to his feet, straightening his long legs. Holding the cocked Colt out in front of him, he moved forward. He glanced at the first door on his left but then shifted his gaze back to the right. A smear of blood shone on the wainscoting on that side of the hall. There was another smear near the last door on the right, which opened suddenly.

A fist clenched around a gun handle was thrust

through the opening, and then Laughing Lyle's snarling countenance appeared above and behind it. The killer had Longarm dead to rights. The lawman threw himself sideways into the nearest closed door as Laughing Lyle's pistol roared, stabbing smoke and flames.

The door gave easily beneath the lawman's muscular bulk, and Longarm's momentum hurled him into the room. He hit the floor and rolled up against a brass-framed bed upon which a young blonde was cowering, bedcovers pulled up to her chin. Her eyes were wide as saucers.

"Get out!" she screamed. "Get out, you brigand! Leave me *alone!*"

Longarm pushed up on an elbow and swung his head toward the door just as Laughing Lyle appeared, long, thin blond hair dancing around under the killer's bald, bullet-shaped pate, thick pink lips peeled back from large, square, grime-crusted teeth as he extended the Smithy once more.

Longarm raised the Colt. It danced and thundered twice. Laughing Lyle jerked back and fired his Colt into an oil painting on the wall to Longarm's right, knocking the picture askew while the blonde screamed and writhed beneath her bedcovers. Laughing Lyle stumbled back out of sight, boots thumping on the hall floor.

Longarm pushed up off his right elbow, then winced as a throbbing pain lanced his arm. He fell back against the bed and looked at the aching wing. The sleeve of his frock coat was torn about six inches down from the shoulder, and blood oozed from the wound. One of Laughing Lyle's bullets must have pinked him in the hall.

The loud boot thuds fell silent, only to be replaced

by a bellowing laugh and the screech of breaking glass. Longarm scrambled to his feet and dashed into the hall just as a heavy *thud* and a grunt sounded outside the broken window. The red curtains fluttered in the breeze ebbing around the ragged shards.

Longarm ran to the window and looked down past a small, shake-shingled awning to see Laughing Lyle heaving himself to his feet in the yard, hefting a pair of bulging saddlebags over his shoulder.

The brigand lifted his chin toward Longarm. A shrewd smile plucked at his fat lips as he raised the pistol. Longarm jerked his head back behind the window as Laughing Lyle's Colt barked twice, flinging lead through the broken window and into the hall ceiling over Longarm's head.

Foot thuds sounded. Longarm looked out once more to see Laughing Lyle running, limping and holding his right arm close against his side, toward the front of the roadhouse. The outlaw's thin, straw-colored hair danced around the bald top of his head.

Longarm threw himself to the left side of the window, and started to raise the Colt in his right hand, but the wounded arm felt as though a rabid cur were tearing into it. He couldn't get the pistol aimed even chest high. He took the gun in his left hand, but by the time he got it aimed, Laughing Lyle had disappeared around the front of the roadhouse.

"Shit!"

Longarm wheeled and, clutching the Colt in his left hand and letting the wounded right arm hang straight down at his side, ran down the hall. He dropped down the stairs two steps at a time, wincing as each jarring step caused the rabid dog to take another hungry bite out of the wounded wing.

The half-breed barman and the three waddies were standing around behind the bar, looking like scolded schoolboys. One ducked with a start when he saw Longarm, who yelled, "Stay where you are, fellas!"

The whore had begun to dress but now lurched back against the fainting couch, holding a corset bustier across her pillowy breasts. "You, too, miss!" Longarm added as he sprinted along the bar.

"What in *tarnation!*" shouted one of the punchers.

Longarm heard hoof thuds in the yard as he approached the closed winter doors. He pulled the doors open and bulled through the batwings in time to see Laughing Lyle galloping westward out of the yard on a white-socked chestnut, bulging saddlebags that contained sixteen thousand dollars in Stoneville loot draped across the horse's hindquarters.

The lawman leaped down the porch steps into the yard, cursing at the ache that the move kicked up in his arm, and raised the Colt in his left hand. He eased the tension in his trigger finger, however. Laughing Lyle was a good seventy yards away and galloping fast, horse and rider silhouetted against a colorful western sunset, behind the shadows of sawtooth mountains.

Boots pounded the porch behind Longarm, who glanced behind to see one of the waddies step cautiously out of the roadhouse, looking toward the dwindling hoof thuds. He swung his gaze to the horses, including Longarm's gray, prancing around nervously at the hitch rack.

"Hey!" the waddie said, pointing toward Laughing Lyle, "he's run off with your hoss, Merle!"

As the other two came stomping out of the roadhouse behind the first man, Longarm holstered his Colt and dug a neckerchief out of his coat pocket. Staring toward Laughing Lyle's quickly diminishing, jouncing figure, frustration biting him now as fiercely as the invisible dog chewing into his arm, Longarm wrapped the cloth around the wound.

"Hey!" intoned the waddie called Merle, pointing westward. "He's makin' off with my hoss!"

"Yeah, well that's not all he's got," Longarm said with a snarl, knotting the neckerchief tightly around his arm, gritting his teeth. He glanced at the waddies. "Don't even think about goin' after him," he warned. "The man's a killer, and he'll kill you laughing."

While the waddies regarded him dubiously, he walked over to his dusty gray and untied the reins from the polished pine hitch rail. His inclination was to ride after Laughing Lyle and the Stoneville loot, but that could take some time. First, he had to check on Morgan.

He climbed into the saddle, swung the horse away from the roadhouse and the three waddies milling on the porch, and booted it into a gallop, heading south.

"Hey, you're headin' the wrong direction!" yelled Merle. "My hoss is west!"

When he'd first scouted the roadhouse, Longarm had memorized the route into the hollow where he'd left Case Morgan. The rock- and brush-rimmed depression was a little more difficult to find in the growing darkness, but then he heard the whinny of Case's mount and veered toward it. When he saw Case sitting where he'd left him, Longarm stopped the gray, swung down from the saddle, and dropped the reins.

"Well, I got three of 'em, anyway." He walked toward where Case slumped against the rock. "I'll go after Laughing Lyle first thing . . ." He stopped and looked down at his partner, who sat with his head tipped back against the rock.

Case wasn't moving. His hat lay crown-down beside him. His pewter-streaked, dark brown hair lay matted against his head.

Longarm felt his throat go dry. He crouched beside the older man. Dread thickened his voice. "Case?"

No response.

Longarm placed a hand on the man's chest, but even before he'd detected no heartbeat he'd seen Morgan's deathly pallor and the opaque stare in the half-open eyes. Longarm laced his hands together, elbows on his knees, and lowered his head.

"Goddamnit, Case."

Sorrow racked him. A knot formed in his dry throat, and he felt a wetness in the corners of his eyes. He gritted his teeth, choking back the sudden swell of emotion. Longarm wasn't accustomed to the feeling. He'd lost partners before. What lawman hadn't? He'd grown a thick hide. But losing Case was a particularly hard bone to swallow.

He crouched there beside his dead friend, guilt climbing into his mix of emotions—guilt over not getting Case to a doctor in Albuquerque when he should have. But none of those feelings was going to change the sad, eminently frustrating fact of Case sitting dead before him now.

Morgan had a folding shovel among his gear. Longarm retrieved it from his horse. He also retrieved the lawman's bedroll. The times they'd tracked together over the years, they'd always agreed that if one of them cashed in his chips the other would bury him in his bedroll wherever it was they happened to be. Neither man was married or had any family to speak of, so this way made things simple for both of them.

Longarm unpinned Case's moon-and-star badge from the man's vest and slipped it into his own pocket. When he returned to Denver, he'd send the piece back to Judge Bean in Fort Smith. He eased Case's body out from the rock, lay it flat, and crossed the man's cold hands on his belly. Then he carefully wrapped him in his bedroll and, with a weary sigh, started digging a hole in the sandy soil beside him. When the dog in his arm started barking, he had to pause and tighten the bandage over the wound, then resume digging.

He knew that a shallow grave would suffice. Case wouldn't want him to linger over the burying, especially when he had a bullet-burned arm and a laughing killer running free.

Longarm buried his friend and erected a crude cross made of mesquite branches and rawhide strips from his saddlebags. He pinched his hat brim at the low mound upon which he'd piled rocks to keep predators away for at least a few days, then stepped into his saddle. Trailing Case's copper bottom bay, he rode back into the roadhouse yard.

The windows of the two-story structure with a wooden false façade were lit for the evening. Stars glittered in the sky. Coyotes howled mournfully as though in tune with Longarm's own wretched mood.

The cowpunchers' two remaining horses were gone from the hitch rack. They'd likely headed on back to whatever ranch they worked on, two riding double. The stocky half-breed barman was standing on the porch. Longarm saw by the light from the doors and window flanking the man that he'd dragged the three dead cut-throats out and lined them up on the porch.

"Whose horse?" the half-breed asked, blowing smoke.

"Friend of mine—a lawman these men shot. I buried him back yonder. His horse belongs to the cavalry. I'll be takin' it with me in the morning when I go after Laughing Lyle."

"Laughing Lyle? That's who that was?" The half-breed shook his head darkly. "Damn, I just thought he was a feller who laughed a lot. Didn't know it was *him* his own self!"

"I'd like a room for the night," Longarm said, swinging down from the gray and tossing the reins over the rail.

"Don't normally take overnighters unless they pay for a girl, but I reckon we can make an exception for a lawman."

"I'll be pay for the room, some grub, and a bottle of whiskey. You can have these men's horses. I take it they're in the barn yonder."

"They are."

"You can stable mine in there, too."

"What about them?" The half-breed tossed his head toward the three dead men.

Longarm climbed the steps heavily, wearily, sucking back the pain in his wounded arm. "Roll 'em in a ravine or bury 'em. I don't care." He stopped near the half-breed, plucked a wad of greenbacks poking up out of the stocky man's shirt pocket. "What's this?"

"Money they had on 'em."

"That'll go back to Stoneville. You can have anything else they got on 'em. I'm sure their guns and horses will be worth a few coins."

He moved on into the roadhouse, and stopped. There were five women in the room. Four sitting with a bored air around one table were scantily clad in corsets and net stockings of various colors, feathers in their hair. Doves awaiting the night's business. Longarm recognized the two he'd seen earlier—the blonde from upstairs and the round-faced brunette who'd been fucking Kid McQuade.

The fifth woman he'd never seen before. If he had, he would have remembered. Firelight and lamplight glittered off her low-cut, red velvet gown trimmed with black lace, and on her rich, dark-brown hair flowing back across her slender shoulders. Pearls dangled from her ears, also reflecting the light of the lanterns and a fire snapping in the hearth at the room's rear.

Her face was Indian-featured, with high cheekbones, chocolate eyes, a long, regal nose, and full, rich lips. Her teeth were the same color as her pearls. Her body beneath the close-fitting gown was lush.

"Well, well," she said, leaning back against the bar, chocolate eyes dancing briefly up and down the tall, broad-shouldered figure before her. "So you're the man causing the big ruckus around here."

Chapter 4

When Longarm merely arched a curious brow at the woman, she smiled more broadly and lifted her chin toward the door. "I'm Tegan's sister. He's the apron. We own this place, him and me. Bought it from Finlay two years ago. Tegan said you're a lawman. Do you think, next time, you could do your law work *outside?*"

She and the other girls studied him.

"I do apologize," he said, walking forward and doffing his hat. "Tegan said I could have a room, Miss . . ."

"Alva. Just Alva."

"Should I call you 'Just' or 'Alva'?"

She tilted her head to inspect his arm. "You're gonna need that cleaned. Go on upstairs. Take the last room on the left. Door's open." Alva addressed the four pleasure girls looking all dressed up with nowhere to go, as there were as yet no customers. "Ladies, haul a tub and water upstairs. Fill it full."

"I'd be obliged," Longarm said.

"Don't be," Alva said, her chocolate eyes looking up into his, little sparks dancing in them. "I just don't want you bloodying up the place any more than you already have. It's hard enough keeping the place going way out here without your brand of trouble."

As the girls started moving around behind the bar, Longarm said, "I'm obliged just the same, Miss Alva," and started for the stairs.

"Here."

Longarm turned back. Miss Alva was holding out a bottle. He took it, nodded cordially, continued to the stairs, and began climbing, feeling the heaviness of the day in every step.

Upstairs, he went into the last room on the hall's left side. It was obviously an extra room, with a made bed and an armoire, very neat and unlived in. The walls were paneled in pine, and there was a faint smell of pine resin. A washbasin sat atop a dresser that in turn was capped with an oval-shaped mirror. A moonstone lantern was bracketed to the wall near the dresser. Longarm lifted the mantle and lit the wick, the light instantly shunting shadows this way and that around the small, neat room.

Longarm had no sooner sagged down on the bed and popped the cork on the bottle than the door opened, and two girls came in lugging a high-backed copper bathtub. He paid them no attention but merely began taking liberal pulls on the bottle. It tempered the pain in his arm but did nothing to dull the mental agony of knowing one of his best friends, Case Morgan, lay outside under a few shovelfuls of desert sand and rock.

Two more girls came up with a bucket of water each—one with hot, one with cold. They glanced at him skeptically as they poured the water into the tub, obviously not sure what to make of him, a little afraid of him, then headed out, leaving the door open behind them. Longarm removed his string tie, untied the neckerchief from around his arm, and shrugged out of his coat. He pulled his shirttails out of his pants and lifted the garment as well as his vest straight up over his head, wincing as the shirtsleeve came away from the bloody wound.

He tossed the shirt and the vest into a corner with his tie, then kicked out of his boots and shucked out of his socks, long handles, and pants. Footsteps sounded in the hall. The door came open. The girl who'd been on the fainting couch with Kid McQuade stopped halfway through the door and gasped, another steaming bucket of water in her hands. Her hazel eyes raked over him, widening slightly, lips parting. Another girl poked her head in behind her, frowning. Then she sucked a breath as her eyes took in the tall, broad, well-seasoned naked man standing between the bed and the tub.

Longarm glanced at them, said with an annoyed air, "What—she tryin' to drown me?"

"Miss Alva said to fill it up," said the petite, round-faced brunette, hazel eyes riveted on Longarm's midsection.

"Well, fill it up, then." Longarm took another long pull from the bottle and went back to inspecting his wounded arm, scowling. "Don't tell me you've never seen a naked man before."

The two glanced at each other, shrugged, then hauled their buckets into the room and emptied them into the tub. As they filed out, swinging their hips and shoulders, the second girl, a strawberry blonde with red ribbons in her hair that matched her nude corset bustier, glanced over her shoulder, once more raking Longarm's brawny frame up and down, and said thickly, "Not like you, mister."

Her eyes glinted. She pulled the door closed behind her. In the hall, she and the brunette snickered as they headed for the stairs.

Longarm had been only half-aware of them. He took another long pull from the bottle, then set it on the floor beside the tub and stepped into the water. He winced against the heat and slid down slowly until his butt was resting on the dimpled bottom. Scooping water over his upper right arm, he washed the wound, which was a clean one. The bullet had gone in the front and out the back, likely only grazing the bone. He'd douse it with whiskey, wrap it, get a good night's sleep, and hit the trail after Laughing Lyle first thing in the morning.

One of the girls had set a cake of lye soap on the dresser. He grabbed it, stood, and lathered himself from head to toe. More footsteps sounded in the hall—the *clomp-clomp* of an assured stride. A single knock on his door and before he could respond to it, the door came open.

Alva came in holding a small leather kit in one hand, a bottle and two glasses in the other. She looked at Longarm standing naked and lathered before her, arched a black brow, then came in and kicked the door closed.

"This room's busier'n Larimer Street in Denver on a Saturday night."

He continued running the cake of potash lye around on his chest and under his arms.

Alva stopped in front of the door, brashly appraised

him once more, then set the bottle and glasses on the dresser. Longarm folded himself back down in the tub and splashed water up over his head and shoulders, rinsing. Alva pulled the room's lone chair out from the corner and set it beside the tub. She sat down in it and set the kit on her knees.

"What you got there?"

"Sewing needle and thread."

"The wound'll heal on its own."

"You'll probably get a fistful of dirt in it before it gets a chance to. Just sit back, Marshal. Me and Tegan have only been out here two years, but I've sewn up a good dozen men so far."

Longarm looked up at the severely beautiful planes of her cherry-colored face between long, dark-brown tresses of her silky hair. Like her nose, her chin was at once strong and delicate. "Call me Longarm."

Alva opened the kit and withdrew needle and thread. "Tegan said you buried a partner."

Longarm sank back in the tub and sighed.

"A good man?"

"Yep."

When she'd threaded the sewing needle with catgut, she set the kit on the floor, rose, and, the velvet gown swishing about her long legs, walked over to the dresser. She popped the cork on the bottle. "This is the good stuff."

She filled two glasses and brought one over to Longarm. "Drink up. You'll need it."

Longarm threw back the bourbon, smacked his lips. "Damn good."

"We stocked it for the railroad men looking to put a

spur line through. Probably won't sway them one way or the other, but a man likes a good drink even when he's way out in the tall and uncut."

Longarm looked up at her again, feeling the liquor wash through him, warming him, dulling his aches and pains and softening the edges of his grief. "And a good woman."

Alva nodded as she held his right arm over the tub and doused it with the whiskey from his own bottle. He hissed at the fiery claws digging into the wound. Alva set the bottle down on the floor, then crouched low over his arm, scrutinizing it closely, pressing her half-exposed breasts against his forearm and wrist. Her bosom was warm against his skin.

"We've got the best girls here. Best within a hundred miles, anyway . . ."

"I'll say you do."

"It'll probably be pretty quiet tonight, it being a weeknight, but we have to be ready in case a mule train rolls in."

She looked at him staring at her, then pinched the skin up around his wound and ran the needle through. "I'm not for sale, Longarm."

Longarm gritted his teeth as she started sewing. "Good to know, Alva. 'Cause I don't like payin' for it."

She poked him again, and the corners of her broad, enticing mouth quirked a faintly devilish smile. But when she'd finished sewing him up and had cut the thread and doused the sewn wound once more from the cheap bottle of whiskey, she walked over to the door and turned the key in the lock.

She turned back to him. Her lips were parted. Her

full breasts rose and fell behind the gown. She blinked slowly, then lifted one foot after the other, removing her shoes.

Longarm watched her without expression.

He continued to watch until she'd gracefully removed the gown and her underclothes and stood before him naked, long hair curling around the fullness of her dark-tipped breasts. The flickering, amber lantern cast shadows into her cleavage, angled down across her flat belly, and into the tuft of curly hair between her long, shapely, naturally tan legs.

Longarm's expression must have betrayed his incredulity. Alva hiked a shoulder. "I don't know. I reckon you could use a friend." She took long, leisurely, catlike strides to the bed, drew the covers back, and crawled under them, pulling them up only as far as her belly, leaving her breasts bare.

They sloped slightly to one side, the brown nipples hard and jutting. "And if you'll forgive me for saying so, it's been a long time since I've had a man's stiff rod between my legs."

Longarm felt a shudder of desire ripple up his spine. His heart thudded. He closed his hands over the side of the tub, rose, and dried himself with the towel she'd laid across the back of the chair. Staring down at her, his heart continuing to thud heavily, loins running hot, he ran the towel through his hair. As he sawed it across his back, Alva reached out from the bed and wrapped her hand around his jutting cock.

Instantly, her breasts rose and fell sharply as she breathed harder, raspier. Slowly, she ran her hand from the base of his cock to the head and back again.

Longarm felt his chest rise and fall, his knees quake.

When she'd pumped him gently several times, she scuttled up onto her knees with a girlish little grunt, shook her long, dark hair back from her face, grinned up at him, then leaned out from the side of the bed and touched her tongue to the tip of his swollen member.

A warm, wet lance of desire jetted up the length of his cock to poke his prostate. He shifted his weight back to his heels, clenching his fists at his sides.

"So big," she said, and swirled her tongue along the swollen head. "So big . . . and fine. So . . . fine . . ."

Then she opened her mouth wide and closed it over him. She took him as far back as she could and made little gurgling sounds as she lathered him with her saliva while tickling the underside of his cock with her tongue. She turned her head this way and that, making hungry sucking sounds, getting him good and wet.

Slowly, she pulled her head back. Her lips rose up and over and back from the swollen, purple mushroom head glittering wetly in the lantern light. She swallowed, and raised those smoky, charcoal eyes to his.

"I believe you're ready."

"Oh, yeah," he groaned.

She lay back against her pillow, lifted her knees nearly all the way to her chest, and spread her legs wide, grabbing her ankles to draw them even wider.

The dark pink rose of her vagina blossomed before him, her legs quivering gently with her need.

Longarm climbed onto the bed. As he mounted her, she arched her back. Propped on his outstretched arms, he caressed the delicate, petal-like folds of her snatch with the head of his cock. She groaned, sighed, quivered. She tipped her head back farther, breasts lifting, pointing toward the ceiling, nipples hard as sewing thimbles.

Her swollen breasts rose and fell heavily, a thin sheen of perspiration covering them as the amber light slid back and forth and the flame guttered.

"You know how to torture a girl, Longarm."

As he thrust the head of his cock through the open, pink blossoms, she brought a hand to her mouth. As he thrust his hips against her and drove his cock deep, deep into her, she gave a sob and chomped down on her knuckles, squeezing her eyes closed. "Oh, *God!*"

Chapter 5

Longarm fucked the girl over and over again, desperately, with a passion that bordered on frenzy.

It was an unself-conscious obsession to drive everything else away except for Alva's breasts and lips and clutching wet snatch . . . her toes gently running up and down his legs . . . her hands gently tugging on his hair . . . her guttural groans and love cries . . . as he took her over and over . . .

. . . before finally burying his face between her full, sweat-slick breasts and at last passing out with a great exhalation, letting his last sensation be the salty taste of her deep cleavage against his lips.

He was only half-aware of her sliding out beneath him and his rolling slowly back with a weary groan against the bed, of her lips pressed lightly to his temple as she gently wrapped something soft around his wounded arm. Everything went dark and quiet again after that, until he opened his eyes to the wash of pearl light pushing through the window above the bed.

He sucked a sharp breath through his teeth. His arm throbbed. With a groan, he tossed the covers back and dropped his bare feet to the floor. Both bottles—the cheap stuff and the good stuff—stood on the dresser. There was also a small burlap sack that hadn't been there the night before. A sheet of lined tablet paper lay over the bag. Longarm opened it, tilted it to the light, read the words written in a flowing, feminine hand:

Dearest Longarm:

Take both bottles of whiskey. Use the cheap bottle on the wound, the bourbon for pain. In the bag I packed food for the trail and cotton for rewrapping your arm. Please, Longarm, do not taint our time together by leaving payment.

I will think of you often, remember last night forever.

Alva

Longarm smiled thoughtfully as he lowered the surprisingly literate note. Not many girls with Indian blood were educated well enough to write such a flowing missive. Longarm wished he had time to get to know the woman he knew only as Alva. She likely had an interesting history. But last night, their bodies had done all the talking. Maybe he'd pass this way again sometime.

In the meantime, he threw back several pulls from the bourbon bottle, filing down the sharp teeth of that rabid cur chomping into his arm, and ate one of the three apples that Alva had packed for him with several roast beef sandwiches wrapped in waxed paper. He'd save the sandwiches for later.

His pain and hunger pangs sated, he dressed and slipped quietly out of the roadhouse. In the shadowy barn flanking the place, he saddled his dusty gray and Case Morgan's bay, intending to use Case's mount in relief of the gray, so he could ride twice as hard if he needed to. He doubted that Laughing Lyle, wounded as he was, would have gotten far, but he wasn't taking any chances. The desire to run the killer to ground and return the sixteen thousand dollars that he and his gang had taken from the good people of Stoneville, before murdering a dozen bank patrons and employees in cold blood, was like a fire-breathing dragon inside of him.

All the more so because they'd taken the life of one of his closest friends, one of the best lawmen on the frontier.

He hoped Laughing Lyle hadn't died from his wounds overnight. He wanted to take the man to Denver, put him before a federal judge and jury, and watch him hang in the gallows courtyard behind the Federal Building.

It was a chilly morning, as they tended to be in early October in New Mexico, at about six thousand feet above the sea. The sun's rays spearing over the eastern horizon were not yet offering warmth. Longarm unwrapped his buckskin coat from around his bedroll, pulled it on, returned the bedroll to its place behind the saddle cantle, and closed the barn doors behind him and the horses, whose tails blew in the cool breeze.

The tall lawman swung into the saddle, gave his glance once more to the two-story roadhouse, the magic of last night with Alva reluctant to leave him, then pressed his heels to the gray's flanks. The horses clomped around the saloon and pleasure parlor to where the trail left the yard—two pale wheel ruts jutting westward across the rolling, sage- and piñon-studded desert.

The roadhouse must not have had much business the night before. Only one set of fresh prints scored the trail's left track, the indentations light and crumbly, denoting a galloping mount. Laughing Lyle.

Ignoring the constant ache in his right arm, Longarm booted the army gelding into a fast trot, jerking the bay behind him by its bridle reins. When the sun left the eastern horizon and started climbing the sky behind him, he put the horses into a hard gallop for a quarter mile before resting them for a short time and then started galloping once more.

After an hour, he began sweating beneath the coat, so he stopped the mounts, removed the buckskin, and tied it around his bedroll. While the horses blew and cropped the fescue growing up between sage plants along the sides of the trail, he inspected the single set of prints scoring the trail ahead.

He crouched over one print, removed his right-hand glove, and pressed his index finger into a brown spot in the clay-colored soil. He lifted the finger and inspected the flaky brown substance, smeared it with his thumb until it became red.

Longarm smiled. Laughing Lyle had been losing enough blood that it was dripping onto the trail beneath his horse.

Longarm splashed water into his hat for his own two horses, let them each drink, then corked his canteen and swung into the saddle once more. He continued following Laughing Lyle's tracks for another hour, watched a mountain range rise ahead of him and slightly to his right—an island hulking against the western horizon. It was likely the Organ Range between the Black Range to the south and the Cactus Hills to the north.

Longarm had been through this country a couple of times before, but he couldn't remember any towns. There were a few, small, widely scattered ranches, none of which he'd glimpsed so far today. Laughing Lyle had so far stuck to the trail, which seemed to be heading for the Organs, so he must have had some destination in mind. Maybe the mountains themselves.

Possibly, he hoped to hole up in the rugged reaches and heal well enough to begin spending some of the stolen money that was all his now that the rest of his gang had gone to Glory. If so, Laughing Lyle wouldn't be alone. The Organs were known for hiding outlaws of one stripe or another—desperadoes on the run looking for a rugged place to cool their heels before making a break for Arizona Territory to the south and west, and then possibly Mexico beyond.

Laughing Lyle had slowed Merle's horse down considerably this far out from Finlay's roadhouse, and rarely run it down the stretch of trail that Longarm was currently fogging. The killer must have passed through here late last night, around midnight or later. It must have been cold then, in the lower forties—and cold is hard on a man losing blood.

As Longarm rode through the early afternoon, switching horses every hour or so, he saw only two other people—punchers moving a small herd of cattle about a half a mile south of the trail. He passed a couple of forks in the trail marked with signs announcing distant ranches, but Laughing Lyle's tracks continued along the main line, heading toward the Organ Range looming taller and broader to the west, the still-high sun revealing its rocky lower slopes and talus slides and jutting pinnacles of what appeared sandstone and limestone. Higher up, the slopes were dark green, with forest thinning toward more slides and barren, rocky knobs.

Around Longarm the terrain was rocky and patchy with sage, prickly pear, and willows demarking thin watercourses, and occasional cottonwoods and cedars. He stopped when the twin furrows of a wagon intersected the hoof tracks of Laughing Lyle's stolen horse. Nearby was a large splotch of blood and scuff marks where a man had fallen. There were two sets of footprints, as well— those of a large man in stockmen's boots, and those of a smaller man, or more likely a woman, in small-heeled shoes.

They'd obviously stopped and taken Laughing Lyle aboard their wagon, likely tied his horse to the wagon, and continued on up the trail.

Quickly, Longarm mounted the gray and, leading the bay, gigged it forward, following a broad bend around a short mesa and then up a slope. He rode for another half hour, then checked both horses down when a town appeared ahead of him, the Organ Range looming tall and formidable behind it.

The town was a sprawling, shabby affair—mostly log shacks, plank privies, and pole corrals scattered among the sage and broken red boulders that had long ago tumbled down the steep ridge to the north. The settlement sprawled on a shallow slope dropping from the foot of the mountain toward the valley to the south.

As Longarm continued following the trail, he saw what appeared to be a business district ahead—eight or nine frame buildings with false fronts stretched out along both sides of the trail for no longer than a city block, with plenty of space between them. These business buildings were surrounded by more shacks sitting every which way, showing a lack of any sort of civic planning whatever, as though the whole place was a haphazard, makeshift affair.

There were a few people milling along the raised boardwalks fronting the businesses, with saddled horses standing at hitch racks here and there, still as statues. A couple of horsebackers were just now riding toward Longarm, who'd stopped his own horses to get the lay of the land.

As the two riders rode toward him, their horses kicking up little red dust puffs, Longarm pinched his hat brim affably. Both riders—ranch hands, judging by their dusty homespun clothes and brush-scarred leather chaps—looked right at him without expression, with no sign of acknowledgment whatever.

They continued past him to head off in the direction from which he'd come. Longarm glanced after them, but their reception, or lack thereof, was no surprise. Folks who lived this far off the beaten path were just naturally suspicious of strangers.

He gave his attention to the dirt street before him. The twin wagon furrows were less clear here, where they'd been somewhat obscured by horse and foot traffic, but the wagon's trail was still visible in places. He followed it ahead to where it angled toward a large frame building over whose double doors a sign announced HUMP-ERDINK LIVERY AND UNDERTAKING.

Inside the open double doors a bearded gent was hunkered over a coffin propped on sawhorses and filling the air with the fresh smell of pine resin as he ran a plane over the top of the coffin's left side panel. To his right was a spring wagon with an open tailgate. Inside the wagon lay a dead man with a blanket thrown over him; his stocking feet stuck out the bottom. A big, blue toe poked from the dead man's right gray sock.

Longarm's heart hiccupped its disappointment.

He returned his gaze to the old man planing the coffin, and his voice betrayed his dread. "Who you got in the wagon, friend?"

The oldster, wearing a tangled gray beard that hung down nearly to the paunch pushing out his striped coveralls, leaped back with a start, gasping. "Jumpin' Jesus, would you mind announcing yourself, fella?" His freckled cheeks were bright red above the beard, and two blue eyes glared out from beneath shaggy brows the same color as the beard. "You damn near frightened me right into a goddamn heart stroke!"

"Sorry," Longarm said. "I thought you heard me ride up."

"Well, I didn't! Can't hear as well as I used to, so I would appreciate it if you'd announce yourself next time."

"How can I announce myself if you can't hear?"

The graybeard cupped a hand to his ear. "What's that?"

"Never mind," Longarm said, raising his voice. "Who you got in the wagon there?"

The old man glanced at the wagon, then returned his indignant blue gaze to Longarm. "Slash Hall. Who's askin'?"

"Slash Hall," Longarm said half to himself, feeling better. He'd been sure the man was going to say Laughing Lyle or at least some gent whom someone picked up in a wagon a few hours ago.

"What's that?"

Longarm swung down from his saddle and dropped the gray's and the bay's reins in the dirt. "Mind if I take a look?"

"I asked you what your name was, boy, and don't tell me you answered when I know you didn't. I'm hard of hearin' but I ain't *deaf!*"

Longarm walked over to the end of the wagon. "Custis Long," he said. "Deputy United States marshal."

"*What* did you say?"

"You heard me."

"What's a federal doin' in Nowhere?"

Longarm pulled the blanket down until the dead man's head was revealed. The lawman grimaced at the grisly sight of the badly swollen face that had turned the color of a black eye. Even one ear was swollen as it poked out of the man's shaggy mop of frizzy, gray-brown hair. His lips were puffed up to the size of large thumbs and stretched back from his teeth in a bizarre death grin.

"Good Lord—what happened to him?"

"Been warm the last few days, and ole Slash was ridin' for the Dancing Bar W south of town when his pony threw him into a rattlesnake hole. By the time they managed to fish him out, it was all over but the screamin'. They said he wailed till well past midnight, Slash did. His bunkhouse pards was about to shoot him when he finally expired."

The undertaker, whom Longarm assumed was Humperdink, walked over to stand beside Longarm and stare down at the dead man. "His pards, J. T. Phipps and Bill Williams, brought him to town and pooled their money for a coffin and proper funeral in the church cemetery, with Reverend Henry Todd presidin'. Two more of his friends just rode out after payin' their respects."

"Good of his friends to do that."

Humperdink nodded, then turned to look Longarm up and down. "What's a federal lawman doin' in Nowhere?"

Longarm frowned. "Nowhere? That the name of the town."

"Shore is."

"How come there's no sign sayin' so?"

Humperdink grinned as though he was delighted whenever he got the opportunity to answer that question. "What'd be the point of identifyin' Nowhere since anyone headin' here already knows they're Nowhere whether they know the name of the town or *not?*"

He slapped his thigh and bellowed a laugh.

Longarm waited until the undertaker's raucous laughter had dwindled to chuckling before saying, "I'm here on the trail of the killer and bank robber Laughing Lyle May. I saw where he'd been picked up and—"

"Yeah, he was hauled in early this morning by the Reverend Todd his own self. The reverend and his daughter, Bethany. I hailed a coupla fellas from the Nowhere Saloon, and they carried ole Laughing Lyle up to Doc Bell's office."

"What about his saddlebags?"

"What saddlebags?"

"The saddlebags Laughing Lyle had on him." Longarm regarded the man levelly and pitched his voice with steel. "Couldn't miss 'em, mister—the ones full of stolen bank loot. Sixteen thousand dollars' worth."

Chapter 6

"Now, look here, Marshal—I hope you ain't accusin' me of stealin' stolen money!" intoned Humperdink shrilly, scrunching up his face indignantly. "Why I never stole so much as a penny's worth of hard candy in my whole life!"

Longarm plucked a cheroot from the pocket of his frock coat and bit off the end with frustration. "You mean to tell me he was hauled in here without the saddlebags?"

"Didn't see no saddlebags."

"Where's his horse?"

"In the back paddock."

"How 'bout the gear the horse had on it?"

"Right over there—by the Todds' wagon its own self."

Longarm turned to stare into the musty dimness of the livery barn. A two-seater buggy with a leather canopy was parked against the barn's right wall, tongue drooping. Longarm walked over to it, placed a hand on the left rear wheel—a stout wheel for traveling rough country—and glanced into the buggy's rear seat. A dirty scrap of burlap, obviously cut from a large feed sack, was draped over the leather upholstery. The sack was liberally smeared with blood.

Longarm looked beneath the rear seat and the front seat, and saw no sign of the saddlebags.

Chewing on the unlit cheroot in frustration, he walked over to where a saddle was draped over a stall partition, near a ceiling post hung with moldy tack of every stripe. It was a worn Texas-style saddle with a large horn and tooled, cracked, and brush-scarred skirting. A red-and-white striped blanket hung over the stall partition beneath it.

Longarm placed a hand on the pommel and glanced back at Humperdink still standing off the end of the wagon with the snakebit dead man in it. "This is all that horse had on it?"

"That's right."

Longarm rolled the cheroot around between his teeth. It stood to reason that the cowpuncher, Merle, hadn't outfitted his horse with saddlebags, since he'd just been riding to the roadhouse for a few drinks and possibly a poke. But Longarm very clearly remembered that Laughing Lyle had thrown himself out the second-story roadhouse window with a pair of bulging saddlebags hanging over his left shoulder, and he'd been hightailing it away from the roadhouse with those same saddlebags flopping across the horse, behind Merle's saddle.

Longarm had followed the man's trail closely, and if

Laughing Lyle had left the trace to hide the saddlebags, the lawman would have seen it. That meant the folks who'd picked up Laughing Lyle had taken them.

Longarm wandered over to where Humperdink still stood looking owly near the back of the dead man's buckboard. "A man of the cloth picked up Laughing Lyle?"

"That's right. The Reverend Henry Todd and his daughter, Bethany."

"You saw no saddlebags when they rode in this morning?"

"No, I sure didn't. I hope you're not going to suggest that the Todds took that money." Humperdink gave a caustic chuckle, his bulbous paunch rising and falling like a large bladder flask behind his overalls.

"I reckon I don't know what to suggest."

Movement in the street behind Humperdink caught Longarm's attention. A middle-aged gent in a cream hat, green plaid shirt, and brown leather vest was walking toward him, the mule ears of his boots dancing around his calves. Suspenders held his duck trousers up on his slender hips, and he wore a pistol in a holster over his potbelly that was about the same size as Humperdink's. A cheap five-pointed star, cut from an airtight tin, winked on his vest.

As the town lawman walked toward him, Longarm fired a lucifer on his cartridge belt and lit his nickel cheroot. He was blowing pensive smoke puffs into the still, bright October air out front of the livery barn as the town's lawdog walked up to him, nodded, and said, "Lawman?"

A thin wing of salt-and-pepper hair dangled over his

left brow. An old, pale scar ran beneath his lower lip. His face was long and weathered, his eyes a rheumy brown.

"Custis Long, U.S. deputy marshal out of Denver."

The local lawman extended his hand toward Longarm. "Roscoe Butter, town marshal. Welcome to Nowhere." He smiled as though he was as delighted by the town's name as Humperdink was. When Longarm shook the man's hand but didn't say anything, the Nowhere town marshal jerked a thumb over his shoulder and added, "I had a feelin' a lawman might be shadowin' ole Laughin' Lyle."

"What kind of shape's he in, Butter?"

"Not good. Doc Bell just got done diggin' two bullets out of him, one in his lung, another in a shoulder. Would they be yours?"

"They would. We met up at Finlay's roadhouse last night. I fed the other three members of his gang pills they couldn't digest so well, gave two more to Laughing Lyle."

Butter whistled and shook his head. "So they're all dead, eh? Dix, McQuade . . . even Charlie Embers?"

"I don't doubt that St. Pete's got 'em all out in his woodshed even as we speak." Longarm took a long drag on his cigar and stared toward a two-story adobe-brick building on the opposite side of the street whose shingle announced itself as belonging to DR. WINSLOW H. BELL, M.D. Blowing smoke, he nodded at the medico's office. "I take it Laughing Lyle's over there?"

"Yep, with Doc Bell and Beatrice. That's right."

"He do any talkin'?"

"No, sir. Not a word. Muttered and grumbled as several boys from the Nowhere Saloon, including my deputy, Benji, hauled him out of the Todds' buggy earlier. But he didn't say much of anything except nonsense words. You shot him up purty good. The doc don't think he'll make it to suppertime."

"I'd like to see for myself," Longarm said, blowing another smoke puff and turning to Butter. "He was carrying stolen bank loot from Stoneville, Kansas, when he shot another deputy U.S. marshal—a good friend of mine—and got away from me. But Humperdink says he didn't see any saddlebags when the Todds hauled his sorry ass into town."

Butter hiked a shoulder. "No, I didn't, either. You sure he made off with 'em?"

"Certain sure."

"Must've planted 'em along the trail somewhere," opined Humperdink, who'd gone back to planing the coffin for the snakebit dead man.

"Sure enough," Butter said.

"I don't think so." Longarm flicked ashes off his cigar, watched them fall like snow to the churned dust and straw at his boots. "I kept a pretty close eye on his tracks, and I didn't see where he left the trail. He stuck close to it and rode hard for how badly shot up he was."

That reminded Longarm of something else that had been chewing on him.

"He seemed determined to get here." He looked from the marshal studying him closely to the town spread out before him, only a few people on the broad main street between the rows of false-fronted buildings, a black-

and-white collie hiking a back leg on a hitching post out front of the Nowhere Saloon. "Like he knew the place, maybe thought he could get shelter here in Nowhere."

"Can't imagine why he'd think that," Butter said with an exaggerated chuckle. "No one here would be sorry to hear the news of that gang's demise."

"You knew them, then, I take it?"

"Oh, hell, they been through here many times over the past three years, since them hounds started runnin' together off their damn leashes."

Humperdink straightened from his work, picking curls of pinewood from his plane. "They're all *from* here, you know."

"No, I didn't know that," Longarm said.

Butter plucked his hat from his head and fiddled with the brim curled up close to the low crown. "They might have been raised out here—all four of 'em growin' up out there amongst them rocks and rattlesnakes—but they sure as hell got no reason to feel at home here, not the way they shot up the town every chance they got, harassed the womenfolk. No one here would see any shine in them boys—devils all."

"Not even ole Laughing Lyle's pappy," said Humperdink with a sigh and a quick head shake as he returned to his work once more.

Butter ran a hand through his thin, matted hair, scratched at a dime-sized mole on his temple, and returned the hat to his head. "Yeah, ole Hy May lives up north, in the Organs a ways—if you call it livin'. Got him a little shotgun ranch with his daughter, Jenny, but she does most of the work around the place. Ole Hy—

all he does is . . ." Butter lifted his chin and tipped his thumb to his mouth to indicate a drinking problem.

Longarm nodded slowly, absorbing the information. "Well, whether he was welcome here or not, he must have felt at home here, since he seemed so bound and determined to *get* here. But what I would most like to know is where that stolen bank money ended up."

"Don't be lookin' at me," Humperdink said. "If I had stolen bank loot, you think I'd be sweatin' for the pennies and piss water ole Slash's pards offered me to build a wooden overcoat for his no-good ass?"

Butter said forthrightly, "I can vouch for Mr. Humperdink's integrity and honesty, Marshal Long."

"What about the integrity and honesty of Reverend Todd?"

Humperdink laughed derisively as he planed.

Butter shaped an incredulous scowl. "Good Lord, man! You'd suspect the preacher of taking stolen loot?"

"I'll suspect anyone in this town until that loot is found. It was taken from a good town, and twelve people died when Laughing Lyle and his cohorts locked 'em inside the bank and torched it. I owe it to the citizens of Stoneville, not to mention the family of the murdered folks, to get the money back to them."

"All right, all right," Butter said, holding his hands up. "I understand. I'll do anything in my power to help you recover those saddlebags, Marshal Long."

"In that case, you can call me Longarm," the federal lawman said with an affable nod, taking another drag off the cheroot before returning his attention to the doctor's office. "Now then, how 'bout if we look in on Laughing Lyle?"

"Come on," Butter said, gesturing toward the doctor's place. "I'll introduce you."

Winslow Bell, M.D., was enjoying a late lunch when Butter knocked on the man's door.

"Well, don't expect to get much out of him, Marshal," the doctor told Longarm as he wiped his thick pewter mustache with a checked napkin, then turned back to his rolltop desk, on which sat a plate of roast beef, mashed potatoes, and gravy. "You ripped him up pretty good. I got the bullets out . . ."

The portly medico, dressed in a white shirt, threadbare wool vest, and baggy wool trousers sagged into the Windsor chair behind the desk and glanced toward one of three closed, green-painted doors in his small, shabby office's back wall. "But I don't know what good it did besides wear my old ass out. Like I told Butter, I don't expect him to last till supper. Hell, he might even be dead now. I haven't checked on him since Beatrice brought my dinner down from our living quarters upstairs."

"I'll take a look." Longarm put his cigar out in an ashtray on the doctor's cluttered desk, blew out the last smoke puff, and walked over to the closed door that Bell had indicated.

He turned the knob and went into the room, which still smelled of carbolic acid and arnica and a few medicines Longarm couldn't name. It also smelled of blood, rancid sweat, and the little charcoal brazier glowing in a corner, up near the head of the bed on which Laughing Lyle lay beneath a tattered quilt.

Besides the bed and the brazier, a wooden washstand was the room's only other furnishing.

As Longarm walked over to the bed's left side, Butter walked around to the other side. Both men were holding their hats in their hands, though certainly not out of respect for the killer who lay unconscious before them.

Unconscious but sort of snarling, like a wildcat dreaming of bloody murder . . .

Laughing Lyle's thick, chapped lips moved as he snarled, and his heavy eyelids fluttered. His stringy blond hair hung down the sides of his otherwise bald head, framing his fair-skinned, weathered, unshaven face. His cheeks twitched, the muscles dancing beneath the tawny skin.

Longarm drew the quilt down to get a look at the man's wounds. He'd no sooner revealed the large, bloody bandage wrapped around Lyle's chest and another around his left shoulder, than Laughing Lyle's right hand shot up to wrap around Longarm's wrist.

The killer's eyes snapped wide as he hissed, *"I been waitin' fer you, you son of a bitch!"*

Chapter 7

"That's just the ether talkin'," said the doctor, chuckling as he stood in the doorway behind Longarm, just as the federal lawman clicked his Colt's hammer back, the barrel of which he'd snugged up taut to the underside of Laughing Lyle's chin.

"Gonna . . . gonna gut ya like a damn *pig!*" snarled the killer, just before his eyes rolled back in his head and his head fell back on his pillow. Laughing Lyle loosed a long sigh, thick lips fluttering over his teeth.

The doctor chuckled again. "He done that all through the surgery so's I had to have Beatrice strap him down on the operatin' table. Damn snake is what he is!"

"Whew!" said Marshal Butter, wagging his head. "He sure had me goin'." He looked at Longarm. "Say, you're pretty fast with that six-shooter!"

Longarm drew his own deep breath, his heart slowing back down to a moderate pace, as he depressed the Colt's hammer and returned the pistol to its holster on his left hip. The sudden movement had kicked up the ache in his arm, reminding him that the wound probably needed a fresh dressing and that he could use a couple of pain-stifling belts from Alva's bottle.

"Think you can keep this killer alive, Doc?" Longarm said, turning toward Bell, who was running his napkin across his mouth as he finished chewing. "I'd like to find out what he did with those saddlebags and then I'd like to get him *and* the loot back to Denver."

"I don't know," Bell said. "Ole Laughing Lyle has plenty of venom in him, and sometimes that's enough to get a man through anything short of bein' slow-roasted by the Lipan Apache. But, like I said, you tore him up pretty bad, and while I'll try my darnedest, Marshal Long, I can't *guarantee* that he'll be alive come suppertime."

"I reckon that has to be good enough." Longarm ducked through the doorway as he walked back into the main office, Butter on his heels. He turned to the doctor. "If he comes around, let me know, will you? I'd like to chat with him, for obvious reasons."

"I'll send Benji for you," Bell said, glancing out the front window right of the door. "I'm gonna send him into the backyard to split some wood for me when he's finished sweeping the shit off my boardwalk."

Longarm glanced out the window, where a big man in a shabby black suit coat and bowler hat was wielding a broom, the *snick-snick* sounds rising from the other side of the door. The federal lawman cast a curious glance at Butter. "Benji? Your deputy?"

"Works for me mostly at night," Butter said with a nod. "During the day, Benji's an odd-jobber."

"That kid can split a cord of wood in an hour," Bell said, chuckling as he stared out the window.

With a grunt against the pain in his right arm, Longarm picked up his saddlebags and rifle from where he'd deposited them on a chair near the doctor's front door. "If you don't send for me tonight, Doc, I'll check back with you tomorrow morning."

"Where will you be staying, Marshal Long?"

Longarm donned his hat and arched a brow at Butter.

"I suggest the Organ Range House," Butter said. "Best flophouse in town." The town marshal smiled. "And it's strategically situated right beside the Nowhere Saloon."

"All right, then—that's where I'll be." Longarm nodded at the doctor, then opened the door and stepped out onto the boardwalk, Butter behind him turning to the big, raw-boned young man with the broom.

"Benji, I'd like you to meet Deputy United States Marshal Custis Long. Longarm, meet my one and only deputy town marshal, Benji Vickers."

"Benji." Longarm extended his hand to the big man, who stood about two inches taller than Longarm. The kid was built like a buggy shed, with broad shoulders and hips and a large, fat belly that appeared hard. His face, even as large as it was, was oddly boyish, his eyes uncertain, bashful.

He wore a star on his wool work shirt under the coat, but there was no gun that Longarm could see, merely a wide brown belt securing his wash-worn trousers to his barrel-sized hips.

The deputy/odd-jobber stared a little dubiously at Longarm before he removed one of his big hands from the broom handle, wrapped it loosely around Longarm's, and gave the marshal's hand a barely detectible squeeze and a shake before releasing it and wrapping his own once more around the broom. A strangely fishy shake for a man so large and obviously powerful.

Shyly averting his gaze, Benji dipped his chin and said softly, "Howdy-do."

"Not bad, Benji," Longarm said. "How 'bout yourself?"

The big boy-man merely spat to one side and resumed sweeping the boardwalk. Flushing a little with embarrassment, Butter stepped into the street. When Longarm was beside him, he tipped his head toward the federal lawman and said softly, "Not a big talker, Benji, but one hell of a deputy."

"I noticed he wasn't armed."

"Doesn't need to be armed," Butter said. "He can break up a saloon fight with his hands alone. Did you see the size of his arms?" Butter chuckled. "Can I interest you in an early supper, Longarm? The Organ Range has a right respectable kitchen for a town so far off the beaten path."

"Don't mind if I do." In the corner of his eye, Longarm noticed Benji watching him furtively while continuing to run the broom across the boardwalk. "But I'd like to get a room first and freshen up a bit."

"Sounds good. I'd like to take care of some paperwork back at the office. Meet you in the dining room in a half hour?"

"A half hour oughta do it," Longarm said, hiking his saddlebags a little higher on his shoulder.

"All right, then."

Butter nodded, then started walking west along the street, toward the town marshal's office a block away, the mule ears of his boots jostling about his calves. As Longarm angled toward the Organ Range House on the street's opposite side and east about fifty yards, he glanced behind him once more. Benji was watching him with a brooding, furtive air; though, seeing that he'd been discovered, the big man-child turned his head away sharply and started sweeping with more vigor.

He had no idea why, aside from that fishy handshake and those furtive stares, but as he angled toward the Organ Range House, by far the grandest building on Nowhere's main street, Longarm made a mental note to keep an eye on the big man. The Organ Range stood a full three stories high and was painted a gaudy amber and green, with a white second-floor balcony rail and several loafer's benches and two comfortable-looking wicker chairs on the pillared verandah.

Large, stylish indigo letters announced the hotel's name on the false façade rising above the third story. The opulence of the place bespoke an optimism its founder must have at one time felt regarding Nowhere's future—an optimism that had likely dulled along with the House's chipping paint and moldering porch pillars. A tumbleweed sat undisturbed on the loafer's bench left of the broad double doors.

Longarm went in and rented a room from a birdlike little woman who kept giving him suspicious, sidelong looks that, coupled with those of Butter's big deputy, started to get on his nerves. When Longarm had paid for two nights in advance—he had a feeling he'd be in Nowhere for a while, waiting for Laughing Lyle to heal, if he didn't expire in the next few hours—she slid a key across her polished mahogany desk but kept her large, somber gray eyes on Longarm. He reached for the key, but she closed her long, withered old hand over it.

Longarm arched a brow at her.

"Lawman?" she said tonelessly.

"That's right," Longarm said. "Federal."

"You here for"—she jerked her chin, shaped like a pistol butt, to indicate the doctor's office—"him?"

"Laughing Lyle. Yes, ma'am."

She lifted her hand from the key and stared down at it gravely. "If you're all by your lonesome, son, you'd best forget about ole Laughing Lyle and ride on out of here while you still can."

Longarm stared at her skeptically. Her demeanor as much as her words caused a prickling of the short hairs at the back of his neck. He was about to ask the little woman to explain herself when a pale, plump young girl in a black serving dress and dusting cap poked her head out of a near doorway and said meekly, "Mordecai would like a word about the roast, Ma."

The old woman glanced up at the tall lawman once more, then strode out from behind her horseshoe-shaped desk to follow the serving girl into the kitchen flanking it. Longarm stared after her for a time. He turned to look out the lobby's front windows into the dusty street that was gathering shadows now as the sun fell.

One horsebacker rode past the hotel at a leisurely pace, leaning out from his horse to spit a wad of chaw into the dirt. He ran the back of his hand across his mustache-mantled mouth as he swung his horse toward the Nowhere Saloon, sitting just east of the hotel.

That made Longarm think of a drink as well as made him conscious of the throbbing in his upper right arm.

He palmed the key, grabbed his rifle and scabbard off the desk before him, and hiking the saddlebags on his left shoulder, started up the stairs to the second story. Room five was on the right side of the hall trimmed with a flowered runner, bracket lamps, and the same green paint that decorated the House's exterior, though the knots in the cheap pine paneling showed through.

Longarm went in, tossed his gear on the bed, sagged onto the edge of the cornshuck mattress, and tossed back a long pull from Alva's bourbon bottle. The only thing that could beat a slug of good Kentucky bourbon was his preferred Maryland rye, but it wasn't often he could find the stuff beyond Denver or a like-sized city. He took another drink, then shrugged out of his frock coat and his shirt, and went to work undressing his wound.

As he did, he thought about the words of warning that the birdlike proprietor of the Organ Range had offered him downstairs. He thought about Laughing Lyle and the missing saddlebags and Town Marshal Butter and then about the big deputy town marshal, Benji Vickers.

What strange, menacing looks the mountain-sized boy had given Longarm. . . .

Why?

The only conclusion the federal badge-toter could come to as he poured cheap whiskey over his expertly sewn wound, letting it run off into a washbowl atop the stand beside the bed, was that someone here in Nowhere knew more about those saddlebags than they were letting on. True, Benji could just be suspicious of strangers, but Longarm felt the kid's odd demeanor was due to the stolen loot.

Which meant that Humperdink, the liveryman/undertaker, or Butter was lying to him, or possibly both.

Or maybe they themselves had been lied to by the Reverend Todd and his daughter, Bethany, who had been the first ones to encounter Laughing Lyle and, ostensibly, the stolen bank loot from Stoneville. Obviously, they were the ones Longarm needed to speak to next.

First, he'd pad out his belly. Just thinking about a plate of food made his stomach grumble. He'd been so immersed in his problems that he'd forgotten how hungry he was. When he'd pulled on his shirt and coat and donned his hat, he glanced at the Winchester. The prickling under his collar told him he might need the long gun before too much time had passed, but he supposed he'd look foolish toting it into the dining room.

He left the gun in its scabbard leaning against the dresser, loosened his Colt in its holster, then stepped into the hall, locking the door and pocketing the small, tarnished silver key. When he'd taken three steps toward the stairs, a latch clicked behind him. He swung around quickly, wrapping his right hand around his Colt's polished walnut grips.

A door on the other side of the hall from his own closed. The latch clicked again. Silence.

The bracket lamps flickered and smoked, rasping ghostly in a vagrant draft scuttling along the hall from the room behind the recently closed door.

Longarm scowled at the door. Whoever was in there was a mite curious about whoever was out here. Natural curiosity or something else?

Longarm turned and continued walking toward the stairs, glancing over his shoulder once more, feeling as though he had a target drawn on his back.

Chapter 8

Butter was already in the dining room, waiting at a table near a front window and a dusty potted palm. There were three other men in the place—traveling drummers, judging by their cheap, gaudy suits, complete with checked or striped trousers and bowler hats with frayed brims.

Butter sat back in a Windsor chair, legs outstretched before him beneath the table, hands laced over his paunch. His cream hat was on the table, which was decked out with a white tablecloth and a green candle in a brass holder. A fire crackled in a fieldstone hearth on the room's far side, compensating for the evening chill.

Night had fallen over Nowhere. The room's three curtained front windows were dark.

Longarm dragged out a chair and sat down, and when the serving girl came, he took Butter's advice and ordered the elk and potatoes with a side order of buttered carrots, and, of course, a beer and a shot of the house's best whiskey.

When the girl had left, Butter frowned across the table at the federal lawman. "You seem troubled, Marshal. Don't worry—we'll find that stolen loot." He fingered the mole at his left temple, rheumy brown eyes regarding Longarm reassuringly. "If Laughing Lyle don't make it, which looks likely, you'll at least have that to take back to Denver. That's the most important thing, anyway, right?"

Longarm had just bit the end off a nickel cheroot and fired a match on his shell belt. Leaning forward with both elbows on the table, he touched the flame to the cigar, and blew smoke into the air above the table. "Tell me something, Marshal—"

"Call me Roscoe."

"All right, Roscoe—tell me about your town here. Tell me about Nowhere."

Butter chuckled. "Don't the name pretty much say it all?"

"What about this hotel? Doesn't look like a place someone would build if they didn't think the town they were buildin' it in had a future. If they didn't think the town wouldn't be *nowhere* for long." Longarm looked around at the lushly if sparsely appointed room, looking past the aged, ragged edges, including the faded quality of the Oriental rug at his feet and the faint coffee stains on the tablecloth before him. "If they didn't think the town would someday be *somewhere*. You get my drift?"

Butter leaned forward, slid his chair up closer to the table, and lifted the whiskey shot the serving girl had just set on the table before him, alongside a frothy, butterscotch-colored ale. He glanced over his left shoulder, then sipped the whiskey, showed his teeth, and said, "See those three men over there?"

Longarm glanced at the three hunkered over their plates and conversing in dry tones, and nodded.

"Railroad surveyors," Butter said, keeping his voice down. "On a survey run for some third-rate railroad that *might* be laid fifteen miles south of here, along Sandy Wash, to connect Albaquerk to the mining camps in the Black Range."

"I'm with you so far."

"About five years ago we had a survey crew moving through Nowhere, and the word was that we were about to have a major line run through here—a line that would connect Albaquerk to us and the mining camps that were just then cropping up in the Organ Range. The line would then head off to the southwest and reach all the way down to Phoenix in the Arizona Territory. So, after all was said and done, Nowhere—this little joke of a town that started out as a cavalry outpost twenty-two years ago and never grew into much since but a supply camp for a handful of small ranches—would be connected to the entire country and the whole Pacific Ocean!"

Butter grinned exaggeratedly, eyes flashing, as he stretched his arms wide, as though to indicate the breadth of the entire planet.

"But it never happened," Longarm said, tapping his cheroot against an ashtray.

"Nope, it sure didn't."

"What happened?"

"No one found enough gold or silver to make the mining camps in the Organ Range profitable, and the rail line that had such big plans and got us all steamed up for wealth and prosperity fell apart on account of a bunch of crooks in their main office in Kansas City. Several o' them mucky-mucks were hauled off to jail. And Nowhere . . ."

Butter scowled down at his shot glass, threw back the rest of the whiskey, and set the glass back on the table, turning it broodingly between his fingers. "Well, the name was just so damn fittin' that we kept it. Now the only surveyors we see through here are workin' for a little narrow-gauge spur line to the south, and those fellas just remind us what could have been."

"Somewhere," Longarm said.

"You got it." Butter laughed gratingly. "So we make a joke out of the name. Why not laugh about it?"

He removed his arms from the table, as did Longarm, for the serving girl had just brought a steaming plate of elk roast for each. She took their beer glasses away for refilling, and the two men dug into the food hungrily.

They'd gotten only halfway through the meal before Longarm saw Benji Vickers's broad, bulky frame fill the doorway that opened onto the hotel's lobby. The big man held his age-silvered bowler in his paws up close to his chest, kneading the brim uncertainly, fidgeting and looking around before he moved forward into the dining room, setting each foot down and wincing, reminding Longarm of nothing so much as the bull in the proverbial china shop.

Butter heard the big deputy's heavy footfalls and looked up, chewing. "What is it, Benji?"

Benji stopped before the table, shifting his deep-set, anxious gaze from the town marshal to Longarm and back again before saying haltingly, "The Widow sent me to fetch you, Marshal. She's havin' trouble gettin' the baby down to sleep and she says she's just fit to be tied!"

Butter's face turned the rose of a summer sunset as he glanced sheepishly at Longarm. He ran his tongue around over his teeth, apparently pondering the situation, before he slid his chair back, tossed his napkin onto the table, and grabbed his hat.

"Longarm, I do apologize, but there's a personal matter I must tend to."

Longarm shrugged—curious but keeping it to himself. "Nothing to apologize for Roscoe. If you gotta go, you gotta go. Shame to leave half a plate of food, though. Perhaps Benji could finish it for you." Why not take the opportunity to have a little sit-down chat with the oddly behaving deputy?

Benji was staring eagerly at the town marshal's food. But as Butter rose from his chair, donned his hat, and made his way around the table, he tugged gently on the big man's arm. "Benji's shift is gonna have to start an hour early, I'm afraid," Butter said. "Come on, Benji. You'd better start makin' the rounds."

Benji wore a pained expression as he dragged his eyes away from Butter's half-finished plate of elk roast, mashed potatoes, and gravy, but he dutifully turned to follow his boss on out of the dining room. Longarm watched them go, then glanced at Butter's plate, twiddling his fork over his own plate, even more puzzled than he'd been a few minutes ago.

Who was "the Widow" and why was she calling Butter away from his supper to tend a child? Was it his own child? Roscoe looked too old to be raising babies.

And what was it that Butter didn't want Longarm possibly finding out from Benji?

Damn, Longarm thought, I'm pret' near gonna have to sit this whole town down and whip them to get any information out of them. But then he remembered his intention of paying a visit to the Reverend Todd's residence, and he resumed shoveling food into his mouth. A clock on the far well read seven-thirty. He didn't want to get over there too late, as the clergy were known for retiring early to say their prayers and read their Bibles.

Or, in this case, possibly to count their money . . . ?

Just as Longarm had scooped the last forkful of potatoes and meat into his mouth and was swabbing the remaining gravy from his plate with a biscuit, the birdlike proprietor strolled over to his table and picked up Marshal Butler's half-empty plate.

"The marshal was called away again?" she said in her leathery rasp.

"I reckon he was. That a habit of his?"

"Oh, I wouldn't know," she said quickly.

The old woman, whom the serving girl had called Ma, set the marshal's beer schooner and whiskey glass atop the plate and began to turn away.

"Oh, I think you might, Mrs. . . ."

She turned back to the federal lawman, pinching her thin lips together beneath a very slight mustache, just visible in the shadows shunted by the room's oil lamps. "Marcus. Margaret Marcus, but most folks call me Ma on account o' I'm so old. Funny thing is I don't have any kids of my own."

She started to walk away again, and Longarm quickly wiped his mouth with his napkin and held her back with

"Ma, I sure wish you'd be a little more specific about your warning earlier."

She stopped and glanced cautiously around the room. A few more people had come in and were eating and conversing, raising a low hum, but none appeared to have overheard what Longarm said. She turned back to him, her gaunt, powdery cheeks flushing slightly, blinking her eyes slowly, portentously. "I said all you need to hear, Marshal, and that advice stands. Would you like to pay for the meal now, or shall I add it to your bill?"

A quick glance toward Butter's side of the table told him the town marshal hadn't left any money for his own food. Had he been in too big of a hurry or was he just the cheap sort?

"Add it." Longarm rose, donned his hat, and adjusted the gun on his hip as the old woman reached for his empty plate. "How 'bout if you point me in the direction of the Reverend Todd's residence? That wouldn't be too much information, would it?"

"Little red shack on Third Street, just south of Norvald's Six-Shooter Saloon," she said, shuffling toward the kitchen's swinging door with the empty dishes. "Go with God, Marshal," she added amusedly as she disappeared into the kitchen. Or, at least, that's what Longarm thought he'd heard her say beneath the clattering of pans in the kitchen and the hum of various conversations around him.

Again, he adjusted his pistol on his hip and glanced around him skeptically. Several pairs of eyes quickly turned away from him. Feeling that uneasy stirring of his short hairs again, he headed on out of the hotel and onto the broad front veranda, the cool evening air push-

ing against him and filling his nose with the smell of
burning piñon pine and the cinnamon tang of mountain
sage.

The town's few saloons were easily identified by the
lights in their windows and the horses nosed up to their
hitch racks. From one of them to Longarm's left emanated the muffled tinkling of a piano.

He'd seen the sign for Third Street earlier, so he
looked around carefully, then stepped down off the
veranda and began angling west across the main drag,
before turning south on Third Street, which was the last
of only three cross streets in the little town. It was eerily
dark out here, the black shapes of both short and tall
buildings and stables hulking around him.

The darkness was tempered by the crisp light of the
stars and, as Longarm continued walking, the lamplight
of a distant building on the street's right side. It was
Norvald's Six-Shooter Saloon, which was a tiny, adobe
brick place with a brush roof and crumbling veranda
and only two saddle horses tied to the hitch rack.

Both horses regarded Longarm curiously, angling
looks behind them, as he continued south to where the
town began to play out. Before it did, a little red shack
slumped at the lip of a deep ravine that curved in from
the south and then ran west behind the little place, which
wasn't much larger than the Six-Shooter but which had
a small second story perched precariously atop the
first one.

There was a picket fence around the front yard, but
it was lacking a gate, as well as more than a few pickets.
Longarm tramped up the worn path through spindly
clumps of sage and buckbrush. A faint amber light

burned in an upstairs window over the porch, and there was another, dimmer lamp lit in a large, first-story window to the left of the front door.

Longarm's boots squawked on the loose boards of the six-by-six-foot stoop, atop which stood a rusting corrugated tin washtub. An unseen cat gave an indignant meow, and Longarm heard the little, padded feet scampering off across the stoop and the light *thump* as the frightened beast leaped into the yard.

He drew open the screen door and was about to knock on the inside door when he heard the crunch of a weed and the ratcheting click of a gun hammer to the left. A snarling voice said, "Best say your prayers, you bastard, because you're about to be blown to *hell!*"

Chapter 9

Longarm slowly lowered his right hand as he turned his head to the left, where a figure stood in the yard aiming a pistol at him over the porch rail. Starlight shone in long, blond hair and on the gun's blue barrel.

"I haven't said a prayer in a month of Sundays," he said. "Perhaps you could teach me one . . . uh . . . Miss Todd . . . ?"

The girl was mostly in silhouette, wearing some kind of bulky coat, but he could see her nostrils flaring as she spat out, "Who the *fuck* are you, and just what in the *fuck* do you think you're doing—skulking around out here in the middle of the night. Be quick about it. I just love the sound of a gun's roar!"

"Is this quick enough for you? I'm Deputy U.S. Marshal Custis Long out of Denver. So if you trigger that smoke wagon, you'll just be doin' it to hear it roar, but you'll be killing a federal lawman in the bargain. That's a hanging offense. And, pardon me, but did you say 'fuck'?"

The girl didn't say anything.

She depressed the pistol's hammer with a click.

She giggled as she lowered the pistol, and starlight glimmered off her white teeth and her eyes as she smiled. "You won't tell anyone, will you, Marshal? I save the farm talk for men skulking around my house of a night when my pa, the good Reverend, isn't here."

"They do that often, do they?"

"Often enough that I keep Pa's pistol loaded and on my night table with my Bible. Well, well, I've been expecting you."

"You have?"

"Oh, yeah. Word travels fast in Nowhere." She ducked under the railing and stepped up onto the porch. When she straightened, the coat she was wearing—an old, molting buffalo robe—flapped open slightly. Longarm caught a glimpse of creamy, jostling flesh. Lightning forked in his loins automatically.

But he couldn't have seen what he thought he'd seen. The preacher's daughter couldn't be naked beneath her robe. But then he hadn't expected a minister's daughter to curse like a muleskinner, either.

"Whoops!" She folded the robe closed across her breasts, and giggled once more. "Yes, I've been expecting you," she said, sidling past him, opening the screen door and pushing through the inside one. Around her was the faint odor of liquor. "Come on in. If anyone slipped inside while I was prowling around looking for whoever knocked over a stack of wood behind the house, no doubt trying to get a look through my bedroom window, you can shoot them for me in the name of the law."

"All right—I'll do that."

He went in and closed the door behind him. The house was small but neat. A lamp burned on the wall that divided the small kitchen to the right from a living area to the left. Stairs rising to the second story split the house in two.

The living room was dominated by a large hearth in which the coals of a recent fire glowed umber. The sparse furnishings included a rocking chair near the fireplace, with a small table beside it, and a horsehide sofa against the wall to Longarm's left, facing the chair and the hearth. There were a few bookshelves and oval-framed daguerreotypes. The air smelled of old pipe tobacco and coffee, and another scent—light cherry perfume, talcum, and brandy—that grew stronger as the girl passed him and strode into the room. She turned up a small, green-shaded lamp on the table and then plopped casually down on the sofa, lounging on her side and drawing her bare knees up toward her belly. When the coat had slid open, he thought he'd been given—accidentally, of course—a brief glimpse of the darker triangular area between her thighs and beneath her belly button.

The light shone golden in her blond hair, which hung in a sexy tangle about her fair, plump cheeks and green eyes. Her small, pink feet were perfectly proportioned.

"Have a seat, Marshal." Her voice was as light and sonorous as glass chimes.

Longarm doffed his hat and crossed the room to the rocking chair. "Miss Todd, I presume?"

"You presume correct, sir," she said with a slightly

jeering, teasing air. "Call me Beth." She rolled her spar-
kling green eyes up and down his long, lean, broad-
shouldered frame. "Damn, you're tall!"

"The farm talk again."

She feigned a gasp and closed her hand over her
mouth. "Oh, what the hell—you already heard me curse.
Would you like a drink? Don't tell anyone, but I tend to
tipple when Daddy's away, and he's away tonight. All
night. Edna Thomas's funeral is tomorrow out at the
Triple 8 Ranch, and he decided to travel as far as the
Spring Creek Ranch to cut his travel tomorrow in half.
I'm not allowed to have boys over—as if there were any
boys around Nowhere I'd *deign* to have over—so you're
technically not allowed to be here. But since you're a
lawman and all, I'm probably safe. You reckon?"

Longarm let his gaze drift up from her bare feet to
her knees. Then it scuttled up the robe to where it was
open just enough across her chest to reveal the inside
curves of her creamy breasts. He looked at her face. She
blinked slowly, obviously knowing exactly what she was
doing to him.

"You bet," he said, easing down into the leather-
padded rocking chair. "But I'll forgo the drink. I'm here
about the saddlebags that Laughing Lyle May was toting when you and your father picked him up on the trail
out yonder."

She arched a brow and stuck the tip of her tongue
between her pouting lips. "Would you like to search
me?" She smiled and wagged a knee.

Longarm bit back a hunger pang. It wasn't a hunger
for food, however. His throat was a little dry. He cleared
it, and put some steel in his voice as he said, "Miss Todd,

the money is nothing to fool about. It was stolen from a bank in Stoneville, Kansas. After Laughing Lyle's bunch stole it, they locked up the employees and patrons in the bank and burned it down. That money belongs to their families and to the town of Stoneville, and I aim to get it back to them."

She sat up and dropped her feet to the floor. Her expression was suddenly serious, sad, and she didn't say anything for nearly half a minute before: "That's just awful."

Her sudden change of demeanor caught Longarm off-guard. It seemed genuine. He said, "Yes, it is."

"Well, I don't know anything about any saddlebags. Father and I only saw Laughing Lyle himself layin' there in the trail. His horse was nearby, grazing, but it was only wearing a bridle, saddle, and blanket. Lyle must have hid the bank money somewhere before he passed out."

Longarm stared at her—just her eyes this time, though the robe was still partly open and her legs were still nearly bare, of course. Only a hardened outlaw could manufacture an expression as genuine and honest-looking as the one Miss Bethany Todd was wearing right now.

Longarm sighed.

"I'm sorry," she said. "I do hope you find the money, Marshal Long."

She rolled her eyes toward the neatly but sparsely outfitted kitchen, dominated by a black range and a square table covered with a green gingham oilcloth. There weren't many dishes on the shelves. The only wall hanging was an oil painting of Christ praying at a small, rough-hewn table. "Before my intruder disturbed me, I was enjoying a bottle of brandy. If you promise not tell anyone of my vices"—she mashed one of her sexy little feet down atop the other and let the robe fall open a little farther—"I'll share some with you."

Longarm felt his throat swell. The lamplight shone on her beautifully, highlighting every other strand in her blond hair, flashing in her green eyes that appeared speckled with copper. Her face was heart-shaped, with a slender nose and rich, red lips. Her chin jutted just far enough, and there was a dimple in it, with a very small mole beside it and a quarter inch below.

Longarm let his eyes travel down the robe once more, and swallowed. It was an almost painful maneuver because of that hard cork in his throat. "Miss Todd, I believe I'd best leave now."

She smiled knowingly, her eyes glinting jeeringly again. "All right. Go, then." It was like a challenge.

Longarm sat like a dead, throbbing weight in the chair that he supposed was mostly used by the girl's father. He stared at her, trying to press his hands down on the chair's worn arms and hoist himself to his feet.

But he couldn't do it.

"You must get lonely here in Nowhere, Miss Bethany."

"Don't I know!"

"You must have plenty of suitors."

"There aren't many young men my age around. Oh, a few from the ranches come in with a spray of wild-flowers from time to time, but it's hard to enjoy a man's company when everyone, including my own father, keeps such a sharp on eye me. I've never gotten that interested in any one man to invite him over, like you're here with me now."

She blinked slowly, her twinkling jade gaze riveted on Longarm. She touched her tongue lightly to her upper lip before adding, "Alone."

Longarm watched her bosoms rise and fall slowly behind the robe that now fully exposed her cleavage and almost the entire right breast except the nipple.

"You can't tell me you haven't . . ."

"Of course I have. A few times. But never to my satisfaction. Sometimes I find myself alone upstairs, just me and my brandy, and I start thinkin' about what it would be like with a real man . . . a large man with experience . . . one who knew his way around a girl's body . . ."

Color rose in her cheeks. She lifted her chin and drew a deep, calming breath, letting her gaze flick down lower on Longarm's big frame. ". . . and I just get so damn horny I feel like I could go out and fuck one of the stallions in Humperdink's back paddock."

Longarm felt as though forked lightning had struck deep in his loins. He repressed a shudder. She smiled, knowing exactly the effect she was having. She wet her lips with her tongue and said very quietly, "Are you sure you wouldn't reconsider having a drink with me?"

"Why not?" he managed to rake out. Even to his own ears, it sounded like someone else locked in the kitchen's tiny pantry.

"I left the bottle upstairs in my room. Warmer up there; I have a fire burning." Bethany rose from the sofa and strode gracefully toward the stairs, tossing her hair down one shoulder and giving him a devilishly coquettish look, her eyes flicking over his groin. "If you think you can manage it, I'll meet you up there."

Longarm watched her disappear up the stairs. The girl was right. His pants were getting tight across the crotch, so he had to sort of turn to one side before hoisting himself out of the chair. He adjusted the twill, trying to drag some slack up from his thighs, then tossed his hat down on the sofa and climbed the short, steep stairs.

He turned at the top. There were two doors, a stretch of pine-paneled wall between them, on which a single wooden crucifix hung. The door on the right was open. Longarm walked to it and stopped in the doorway.

Bethany stood in front of the small bed in the room, which wasn't much larger than a sleeping compartment in a Pullman car. She faced him, the buffalo robe now hanging open. The girl lifted her shoulders, shook her creamy, pale body, and the coat dropped to the floor with a quiet, breathy *whump*.

Her body was delectable, arms and legs slender, belly slightly rounded like her thighs, full breasts standing up proudly on her chest, pink nipples pebbled. The light from a nearby coal brazier flickered like liquid bronze across her from the side, raking her and the wall on the opposite of her with curving shadows.

"You like what you see, Marshal?"

"What's not to like?" Longarm shrugged out of his frock coat and kicked out of his boots, keeping his eyes on the delightful, blond-headed vixen with green, glowing eyes before him. Along with the smell of the coal smoke, he could smell the musky need of her. It seemed to radiate from her breasts and the thatch of glistening blond hair beneath her belly.

When he was naked, he walked to her. Her eyes widened, gained an almost apprehensive cast as she stared at the piston-hard shaft jutting at a forty-five degree angle above his belly, the mushroom head swollen and nodding.

"Oh, my . . . God!" she whispered, dropping to her knees as though in worship before him.

She stared at the raging hard-on, the light of the fire flickering in her wide eyes. Slowly, she raised her arms and wrapped her hands around him, then slid her head forward, stuck out her tongue, and touched it to the base of his organ. Even more slowly, she ran her tongue up the underside of his shaft to its head, which she kissed passionately, giving a little cry from down deep in her throat.

Holding the shaft in her hands, she looked up past it into his eyes. "Oh . . . *my* . . . !"

"Call me Longarm."

She rose, pressed her hands against his broad chest, and ran them in a swirling motion down across his belly. Longarm drew her to him and kissed her.

They kissed for a long time, and he savored the sweetness of her little wet tongue flicking against his own teasingly, further stirring the fires inside him. He massaged her firm breasts, feeling the pebbled cherry nipples raking his palms. As he did, she rubbed her snatch against his cock, squirming and groaning.

Finally, she pulled away from him, turned, and dropped to her hands and knees on the bed. She slung her hair back across her neck and looked over her shoulder at him, sticking her naked ass toward him with the little furry pouch showing beneath it, glistening in the light from the brazier, waiting . . .

He walked over to her, grabbed her hips, and slid his cock slowly, gently inside her. Twenty minutes later, cupping her breasts in his hands as he hammered his hips against her ass, he gnashed his teeth against her high-pitched, keening cry of ecstasy.

Chapter 10

"Tell me about the marshal here in Nowhere," Longarm said as, lounging abed with the preacher's daughter, he sipped from his brandy glass. "Tell me about old Roscoe Butter."

He sat with his back against the headboard, naked beneath the wash-worn sheets and one tattered quilt. Bethany lay against him, her own naked body warm and smooth, her head on his belly. With one hand, she was gently stroking his balls. He could feel the slight prickling of her still-damp crotch against his thigh.

"What would you like to know about him?"

He took another sip from his glass, then groaned at the magic her fingers were working beneath his belly. He drew a calming breath. "When we were supping in the hotel earlier, his deputy came in and fetched him. Said something about a widow needing his help with a fussy child."

"Hetta Broken Bow," Bethany said with a fateful

sigh. "Everyone calls her the Widow since her husband, Early, got drunk and fell off his mule out front of the Nowhere Saloon. He hit his head on the stock trough, broke his neck. It's common knowledge that, while Butter isn't married to the woman, he fathered the Widow's latest child. The Widow's three children are all from different men.

"She's a half-breed and lives up on the north side of town and raises those urchins with her mother, Rosa. Her mother's sick most of the time, so she calls on Butter often to help with the kids. He goes because if he doesn't, Hetta'll come for him herself and raise holy hell in front of the whole town."

"Nothin' so scandalous in that, I reckon—aside from them not bein' hitched." Longarm was aware of many men who'd fathered children out of wedlock.

"Well, there wouldn't be," Bethany said, closing her rich lips over the side of Longarm's glass, taking a sip, and swallowing, "if Butter wasn't already married to a former percentage gal who isn't all that happy about the setup and complains around town about it when she's drunk on cheap whiskey."

"Ah, I see," Longarm said, gently sliding a lock of honey-blond hair back from Bethany's incredibly smooth cheek. As she resumed lightly running the tips of her fingers across his balls, he groaned and added, "Butter has himself wedged between a rock and a prickly pear cactus."

"I feel sorry for him personally. Just an old cow-puncher off one of the ranches around here; came to town when he got too old to wrestle steers, and someone pinned that badge on his vest." She looked up at him, hair sliding like silk across his belly. "Why do you ask, Longarm?"

He stared across the room, beyond the sphere of light being thrown by the lamp on the small table beside him. "Just tryin' to figure out who has the most cause to run off with stolen bank money."

"Honey, I told you," Bethany said huskily, looking up at him in admonishment from beneath her brows, "Papa and I found no money on Laughing Lyle. If he ever had those saddlebags, he *had* to have buried them somewhere along the trail before we found him."

Longarm looked down at her smiling up at him angelically, breasts sloping toward his chest, her nipples mashed against him. He could feel the heat in the delicious twin mounds. She was running her hand over the head of his cock, gently tickling, causing it to swell. Amid his growing desire, a question blossomed.

Was she telling the truth about the saddlebags, or was she toying with him? Had tonight been more about pleasing *him* physically and thereby distracting him from his suspicions of her and her father? Or was she really just an overly confined young lady badly in need of having her ashes hauled?

She must have been reading his mind. She pressed her lips to his belly, then scuttled up on top of him, straddling him and sliding her face up close to his, while gently tugging on his ears. "You don't still think *I* have them, do you?"

"Nah, I reckon not," he lied.

She giggled. He felt her pussy against his member, which, he now realized, was hard and jutting once more.

"You know what I think, Longarm?" she whispered

in his right ear, his cock growing even harder as he felt the warmth of her breath and then the wetness of her tongue licking him.

"What's that, Bethany?" he said, watching as she reached between her hips and wrapped her hand around his cock.

"I think you need to take the rest of the night off from thinking about those saddlebags and give me another hard rutting!"

"You think so, do you?" His voice was a ragged growl in his chest. He watched as she rose up on her knees, the lamplight glistening on her snatch. She slid the head of his cock against it a couple of times, opening the folds and breathing hard, pale breasts swaying above him, pink nipples becoming ripe cherries again.

"Yes, I certainly do," she said, groaning as she dropped her snatch down over his cock.

He felt himself sliding up inside her warm wetness. His heart hiccupped.

He ground his fists into the sheets.

She began raising and lowering herself, her hair buffeted, breasts sliding to and fro, nipples raking him gently.

"You know what, Bethany?" Longarm asked her, grunting.

"What's that, Longarm?" she said in a tiny little girl's voice.

"I do believe you're right."

An hour later, leaving the preacher's daughter sound asleep and sexually sated at last, Longarm slipped out the little house's back door. He didn't want to be seen leaving her house so late at night, as rumors would fly like lava from a spewing volcano. It was late—nearing midnight—and he doubted anyone would be out and about. But there was no point in taking chances with a girl's reputation.

The night was cool and dark and silent, the stars even brighter than before in that clean, dry, autumn sky.

He walked out into the backyard, shouldered up to a cottonwood tree, and dug a cheroot from his coat pocket. He'd just fished a lucifer match from his pants pocket and was about to rake his thumbnail across it, when he heard something.

He froze.

There was the faint, wooden rattle of logs from the small, open shed ahead of him, where he could see two, waist-high rows of split cordwood and another row that was nearly shoulder-high. A cat meowed shrilly. A man said under his breath, "Fuckin' *cat!*"

Longarm stepped back behind the tree and, holding the cigar in his left hand, slipped his Colt from its holster with the other hand and ratcheted back the hammer. He said softly but pitching his voice with menace, "Who's there?"

Foot thuds sounded from behind the largest of the woodpiles. Someone was running back there—jogging rather. The foot thuds dwindled as the man fled.

"What in hell . . . ?"

Longarm stepped out from behind the cottonwood and started jogging forward, careful not to stumble over something in the darkness. He ran around behind the large woodpile, then followed the sounds of the running feet northward and back toward the heart of Nowhere.

There were several shacks and pens and wagons out here, and a dog started barking somewhere off to Longarm's left.

Most of the cabins were dark, though a few curtained windows glowed weakly. Longarm walked around behind the Six-Shooter Saloon, a couple of whose windows were also wanly lit.

A silhouetted figure stood outside the closed back door between two low windows. A cigarette glowed between his lips. He had his fists on his hips, which were thrust forward. Longarm could hear the unsteady piss stream he was loosing into the yard just off the back step.

The pissing man grunted. "What the hell's goin' on back here, fellas?"

Just then a shadow moved off the Six-Shooter's far corner. Longarm dove to his left as a gun flashed and bellowed. He hit the ground, hearing the bullet plunk into a dilapidated stable behind where he'd been standing a second before. Longarm rolled over and came up firing once, twice, three times at the silhouetted figure crouched off the saloon's corner.

He thought he saw the shooter's shadow jerk slightly before the man threw himself against the building and out of Longarm's field of vision. Meanwhile, the man who'd been pissing had fallen back against the saloon's door, yelling, "Hey! Hey! Hey! What the *fuck?*" He fell drunkenly, cursing and grunting and trying to tuck himself back into his trousers.

Longarm kept his Colt aimed at the saloon's rear corner, ready.

When nearly a minute passed and the bushwhacker did not show himself again, Longarm heaved himself to his feet, keeping his gun aimed. He began jogging toward the place from which the shooter had fired on him, glancing at the drunk still fumbling with his fly buttons and cursing indignantly.

"Did you see who that was?" Longarm asked.

The man only grunted and cursed. Longarm ran around the saloon corner, extending the Colt straight out in front of him. Nothing there but shadows cast by the adobe brick saloon wall and strewn trash.

In the street beyond the saloon, a shadow moved. Boots thumped in the dirt, and a man was breathing raspily. Longarm ran down along the side of the building and into the street, angling toward a side street in the direction the shadow had gone.

He lost the man in the shadow of another building, but then he caught sight of the shadow again as it swung around the corner onto the main street, heading east. Longarm stopped, breathing hard, holding the Colt straight up in his right hand, hammer cocked. He looked to his right, saw an alley mouth, then headed down it, risking tripping over something in the darkness behind the buildings but wanting to cut the bushwhacker off.

He managed to jog a block eastward along the trash-strewn alley without falling into an exposed privy pit, then made his way back up to the main street by way of a gap between buildings. He dropped to a knee and looked up and down the street.

He turned right in time to see a man walk heavily up the steps of the Nowhere Saloon, which was still brightly lit against the dark night, with six or seven horses still tied to its two hitch racks. The man pushed through the batwings and disappeared inside.

The bushwhacker?

Longarm looked around. There was no one else on the street—at least, no one else he could see, though someone could be crouched in a break between buildings or hunkered down behind a stock trough, waiting to finish what he'd started.

Slowly, looking around carefully, Longarm angled across the street toward the Nowhere Saloon. As he approached, the low hum emanating from inside grew slightly louder. At the bottom of the Nowhere's porch steps, he stopped, took another careful look around, then climbed the steps and stopped in front of the batwings, casting his gaze inside.

A half a dozen men stood along the bar on the room's right side. A few more sat at tables within the glow of the lit lamps hanging near and around the bar. The rear of the place and the room's far left were in darkness.

A fat, fair-skinned barman with a curly mop of hair and a tangled beard was drawing a beer at the bar. He scraped off the foam with a stick, then set the beer in front of a man in a wool-collared denim jacket and brown hat about midway down the bar. Keeping an eye on the man in the denim jacket, Longarm pushed through the batwings.

All eyes turned toward him, and the conversations fizzled. Longarm raked his gaze around the room once more, through a haze of drifting tobacco smoke, then pinched his hat brim to the room in general, said to the fat barman, "Whiskey," and sauntered over to the bar.

He glanced at the man in the denim jacket, who sipped the freshly drawn beer and looked over his shoulder at Longarm. He was a lean, weathered, middle-aged gent with a neatly trimmed mustache beneath broad, sun-reddened nostrils. He didn't seem all that interested in Longarm. But then, all the faces staring at him regarded him with only idle curiosity. By now, most folks in town likely knew who he was and why he was in Nowhere. None of the faces stood out as unduly tense or otherwise suspicious, but something told him the bushwhacker was here, trying to blend in with the crowd.

When the barman had poured the shot, and Longarm had paid for the drink, he picked it up in his left hand, leaving his right hand free, and walked over to a table. He sagged into a chair facing the bar. The other men had returned to their conversations, though the hum didn't climb as high as it had before.

Did the others know who he was after? Or have their suspicions? Of course, he could inquire with the bartender about who had walked into the saloon ahead of him, but doing so might trigger a lead swap in these close confines and endanger the bystanders. Something told him to let the situation play itself out.

At the same time, however, something told him hell was about to pop.

Chapter 11

Longarm slacked back in his chair and sipped his drink, raking his gaze across the men bellying up to the bar and the three who sat at a round table between him and the batwings over which the cool night air drifted.

He'd just taken another sip of his drink when he spotted something on the floor near the bar. A drop of blood fell. Then another to the left of the first, and then another.

The last one was on the floor just right of a dusty black boot. As Longarm stared at the dime-sized blood drop, another one dropped down the inside of a pants leg and glanced off the boot to land beside it. Longarm's eye moved up the yellow-checked trouser leg nearest the blood drops until he saw the face of the man belonging to the trousers staring at him in the back-bar mirror. He was a wizen-faced gent with a steel-colored mustache and frosty blue eyes, long, silver hair hanging down the back of his charcoal-colored wolf coat.

His eyes were shrewdly sharp, jaws taut. Longarm had just snaked his right hand across his belly for his Colt when the man swung around to face him, a Colt Navy .44 in his right hand. Longarm's six-shooter spoke first. The bushwhacker's shot overlapped it, the bullet drilling a chair back on the far side of the table from Longarm, throwing splinters.

As a startled roar lifted from the small crowd, and men flung themselves away from the bushwhacker, the shooter groaned and doubled over, triggering another bullet into the floor in front of his right boot. He dropped to his knees, hat tumbling off his shoulder, and started raising the Colt Navy once more.

"Hold it!" Longarm yelled, wanting the man alive.

"Hold this, you son of a—!"

Longarm shot him again, sending him sprawling, flopping around like a landed fish on the floor fronting the bar, blood pumping from a wound in his lower right side and another in his upper right chest. He tried lifting the pistol yet again, but couldn't get it off the floor. He dropped it, and his shaking hand fell on top of it.

Longarm rose from his chair, keeping his pistol extended. A hush had fallen over the place, all the other customers crouched and shifting their shocked gazes between Longarm and the man on the floor, who was still flopping his arms and kicking his legs, spitting curses out with the blood issuing from his mouth.

Longarm walked over to him and kicked the Colt out of his reach. He glanced at the others, one group clumped to his left, one to his right, with the three men who'd been sitting at the table now standing behind it. Longarm didn't know if any were friends of the shooter's, but he wasn't going to take any chances.

He glanced at the group to his left, and wagged his gun toward his right. "Get on over there with the others, and don't anyone let a hand stray to a pistol, understand? Or you'll get what he got."

When he had all the other patrons grouped near the batwings—except for the barman, who stood behind his bar, fists on his hips and looking none too pleased— Longarm dropped to a knee beside the writhing shooter. The man's long, coarse gray hair slid around his face as he wagged his head from side to side.

"Who sent you to beef me?" Longarm asked him.

"Fuck you!" the dying man roared.

Then he coughed up another gob of blood. His body fell still. He gave a gurgling sigh, and his pale blue eyes stared opaquely up at the saloon's low rafters.

Longarm cursed and straightened, holding his own Colt straight down at his side. He hadn't been sure the man was after him and not just skulking around the Todd house, trying to get a look at Bethany naked. But now he knew. He'd heard it in his words, seen it in his eyes.

Longarm slid his gaze around the onlookers, then gestured at the dead man with his gun. "Who was he?"

No one said anything. They just stared at the dead man.

"Who was he?" Longarm asked again, louder, his patience growing thin.

"Dave Ross," one of the three onlookers who'd been at the table blurted out. "What the hell you kill him for?"

"In case you didn't notice, he tried to kill me. And

that's the second time tonight! What I want to know is who's he workin' for?"

The men looked around at one another, and a dull hum of conversation rose. They all just shook their heads and shrugged their shoulders until the barman said, "Ross is a wolfer. Works for the area ranchers. If he had a beef with you, mister, it musta been personal."

"Personal, bullshit. You men all know why I'm here and what I'm looking for. Saddlebags filled with loot stolen from a bank in Stoneville, Kansas. Don't aim to leave without it."

Longarm's impatience had turned to a burning anger that tightened his shoulders and jaws. Getting bush-whacked just naturally had that effect on him. "Now, anyone else want to try to keep me from locating said loot, make your play." He shoved his six-shooter down tight in its holster and held his hands out away from his hips. "There—I'll even give you half a chance!"

They all just looked at him, as though at a mountain lion hunting too close for comfort. A hush had once more fallen over the room. Obviously, no one was going to try making that play. Reading their eyes, Longarm realized he might have let his temper get away from him. Maybe Dave Ross really had been working on his own, or at least he might not have been working in cahoots with anyone here.

Longarm's head so reeled from frustration that he was late hearing the sound of heavy, running feet and the loudening rasps of labored breath. Boots pounded the gallery fronting the saloon, and then the face of But-ter's deputy, Benji, appeared over the batwings. The big kid's face beneath the narrow brim of his beat-up bowler was swollen and red from exertion. His anxious blue eyes raked the room and then his mouth opened slightly when he saw the dead man flanking Longarm.

Benji pushed through the batwings and moved forward slowly, heavily. "I heard the shootin'." He kept walking toward the dead man, stopped, and turned to Longarm, his voice mild with surprise. "That's Dave Ross." He looked at the gun in Longarm's cross-draw rig. "You shoot him?"

Longarm nodded.

"H-how come?" Benji asked, tilting his hat forward as he scratched the back of his head, staring down at the dead man.

"He tried to beef me earlier outside." For obvious reasons, Longarm didn't want to tell just *where* Ross had tried to beef him the first time. "I followed him here, and he tried it again."

"Why?" Benji said. "What for?"

Longarm scrutinized the big, slightly simple-minded kid—a deputy who wore no gun. "You tell me, son."

Benji swung his big head slowly toward Longarm, scowling in befuddlement—or at least what looked like befuddlement. "How'd I know, Marshal?" Benji's face swelled up even more and turned even redder as he half-sobbed and half-yelled, "Honest to the Lord Jesus, Marshal, I don't know no goddamn thing about *nothin'* around here!"

Then he swung around and ran through the batwings so fast and hard that he nearly tore the doors off their hinges.

Longarm stared after him. Well, if it wasn't one damn puzzling thing after another. He suddenly wanted to do just what Benji had done, and just keep running.

Instead, he turned back to the dead man, knelt beside him, and went through his pockets. He found nothing at all except a receipt for .44 shells and strychnine, a pencil stub, a short grocery list, some pipe tobacco, a corncob pipe, and six dollars in paper money as well as six bits in coin. The man wore another pistol—a Volcanic .30-caliber six-shooter—in the well of his boot, and a little derringer hung inside his shirt from around his neck.

There was nothing that might have told Longarm who had hired the man to bushwhack him—if he'd been hired, that was. If he was working alone, why had he wanted Longarm dead? What had he known about Laughing Lyle's saddlebags?

Longarm doubted very much that Dave Ross was just another owlhoot who harbored a grudge against him as a lawman, because he didn't remember ever having crossed paths with the man before. No, it had to have something to do with Laughing Lyle and the Stoneville loot . . .

He straightened, looked around at the other men in the place regarding him sheepishly in their two separate clumps, the bartender regarding him with disgust from the other side of the bar. Longarm tipped his hat to the barman and headed for the batwings.

"As you were, fellas," he said.

"What about him?" the barman asked.

Longarm glanced back at the dead man, and shrugged. "Send him over to Humperdink's with my regards."

* * *

Longarm tramped heavily over to the Organ Range House next door to the saloon. He tipped his hat to Ma Marcus sitting behind the front desk, crocheting, as he crossed the lobby to the stairs. A mug of coffee smoked on the desk in front of her.

"I heard the shootin' next door," she said. "Not that it's all that uncommon, but I started wondering if I was gonna see you again, Marshal." She chuckled and wagged her head as she continued clicking her needles together.

"Good night to you, too, Ma."

Longarm continued on up the stairs. He slowed as he approached his room, seeing a shadow move under the door just up from it and on the other side of the hall. He was not surprised when the door's latch clicked. Longarm reached across his belly and closed his hand over his Colt's walnut grips and kept his cautious gaze on the door.

There was a slight squawk as the door opened about two inches. An eye appeared in the crack, glittering in the dull light of the flickering bracket lamps. The eye found him, widened. He heard a gasp, and then the door closed.

The latch clicked.

Longarm growled, grinding his teeth, and strode up to the door. He rapped twice on it with his fist, then stepped to the far side lest he should be met with a bullet through the door. "Open up, goddamnit! You wanna get a look at me so goddamn bad, then open up and take your look!"

He slid the Colt from its holster, held it straight up in front of him, and waited, listening.

A floorboard complained on the other side of the door.
The latch clicked. The hinges squawked their familiar
squawk as the door drew open a foot. Nothing happened
for a moment. Then a gun appeared, slowly being thrust
through the opening. An old-model Remington .44.
When Longarm could see the hand holding it, he smashed
his Colt down hard against the barrel.

The hand released it as the owner of the hand
screamed. Longarm stepped in front of the door, shoving it farther open with one hand while thrusting his
hand against the chest of the person he found before him.
He was vaguely surprised to feel the twin mounds of
what could only be breasts under a rough work shirt, and
that the person flying back away from him and hitting
the floor with an indignant groan was a well set-up,
tawny-haired girl.

"Goddamn your eyes!" the girl cried, lifting her head
and tossing the tangle of hair away from her tan, copper-
eyed, heart-shaped face. "You leave me alone, you son
of a bitch!"

Longarm figured she was about Bethany's age.

He stood in the doorway, scowling at her, incredulous.
"Who in hell are you, missy?" His brain was fatigued
from all the questions he'd found himself having to ask.
"And what in the hell were you tryin' to do with that
gun?"

"I was trying to defend myself," she yelled, gritting
her teeth, eyes blazing furiously. A scar across her lower
lip did nothing to temper her earthy, dusky-skinned
beauty. There was a frank, tomboy quality about her,
and a faint, husky rasp in her voice.

"Don't know if I buy it, but that's one answer. Now, who in the hell are you?"

She stared at him, her well-filled dark-blue work shirt rising and falling heavily as she breathed. She swallowed, licked her lips. Her eyes flicked around uncertainly before returning to Longarm. "I'm Jenny May."

When Longarm just stared at her, saying nothing, she added, "I'm Lyle May's sister."

Chapter 12

"Half-sister, I should say," the tawny-haired, brown-eyed girl added quickly, correcting herself.

"Well, now," Longarm said, kicking the door of the girl's room closed. "Ain't this cozy?"

Jenny May gritted her teeth as she glared up at him from the floor. "What in the hell are you talking about?"

"You bein' here for your brother." Longarm poked his hat brim back off his forehead. "If you really are Laughing Lyle's sister. You sure as hell don't look like him."

"We have different mothers."

She started to rise, and Longarm moved forward to help her. She only glared up at him, light brown eyes flashing in the light of a candle atop the room's dresser, and Longarm stepped back with an ironic chuff as she climbed to her feet unassisted. As she did, his male eyes appraised her.

While she was dressed like any trail hand—and an

especially poor one at that in patched denims, work shirt with a tattered collar, a cracked leather belt around her slender waist, and worn men's stockmen's boots probably in a boy's size—she wasn't lacking physically. Her face was earthily beautiful and framed in tawny, sun-bleached hair that hung in thick, curly waves to her shoulders. Her bust was firm and full though not overlarge, and her hips were nicely rounded, legs long and muscular—the legs of a girl accustomed to long hours in a saddle.

"Lyle's mother was a parlor girl, long dead from consumption," she said, throwing her hair back from her collar and standing with one hand on a brass bedpost. "Mine died when I was a year old, of a milk fever." She frowned at him peevishly. "What're you lookin' at?"

"You sure you're Laughing Lyle's sister and this ain't some kind of setup?"

"Why do you ask?"

"Well, you know what he looks like, and I take it you've seen yourself in a mirror a time or two . . ."

If she felt complimented by the comparison, she didn't show it. She only flared her tanned nostrils at him and fired another couple of arrows at him with her eyes. "I've already explained it to you, haven't I?" She crossed her arms on her breasts as though to block his view of them. "Now, would you mind heading back to your room? I'd like to get my pistol and turn in. I'm tired."

"Ah, your pistol. You mean, the one you were going to beef me with?"

"I wasn't going to beef you if you weren't going to pester me."

"What's with all the door clickin'? Why do you keep spyin' on me?"

Jenny's eyes flashed again, brighter. "I wasn't spying on you. I'd heard you were here to take Lyle back to Denver, and I was just curious."

It was Longarm's turn to sneer. "Just about that? Or maybe about the saddlebags your brother was carryin' with him, too?"

"No! I heard about them, of course, but I . . ." She let her voice trail off as light footsteps sounded in the hall. Presently, someone knocked on the door.

Ma Marcus's raspy voice said, "Jenny? You all right in there, honey?"

"I'm all right, Ma. I'd appreciate, however, if you'd inform the lawman here that it's not polite to bust his way into girls' rooms."

Longarm snorted and opened the door wide to see Ma Marcus standing there in a gaudy, high-collared, long-sleeve dress, a Persian cat pressed against her small bosom. Ma arched an eyebrow and looked past Longarm at Jenny.

"You two know each other?" Longarm asked, shifting his gaze from Ma Marcus to Laughing Lyle's sister.

"Of course we know each other," Ma said. "I always put Jenny up here when she and her pa come to town for supplies. Old Hy May likes to dilly-dally for a few days, gamblin' an' cavortin' an' such, and I like Jenny to have a safe place to room while he does. A safe, clean place."

"I came alone this time, waiting on some freight. I was here when Lyle showed up, though I ain't seen him yet. I'm stayin' on account of him, see what happens to him, so I can tell Pa." Jenny walked past Longarm and wrapped an arm around the withered old lady, briefly stroking the cat half-asleep against Ma's spindly shoulder.

"Ma looks after me when I come to Nowhere. She let's me stay here for free."

"Oh, she helps in the kitchen—Jenny does!" Ma said. "Never seen a girl work so hard. I guess she had to learn quick, growin' up out there with ole Hy May." Obviously, Ma didn't approve of the girl's and Laughing Lyle's father.

Jenny squeezed the woman's shoulder, smiling sweetly, and her smile was damn near angelic to Longarm's eyes. What a contrast between her and her brother!

Turning to Longarm but keeping one arm around Ma, Jenny said, "To answer your question, Marshal, I am most certainly not here for the stolen money. Of course I heard about it. Who around Nowhere hasn't? I'm here only for Lyle. Just happened to be here when the Todds hauled him in.

"I sent word to Pa that Lyle is here, wounded, and that I'll haul him home when and if he dies. Pa himself is . . . sick." She made a face before continuing. "Bottle sick, I guess you could say . . . so I'm here alone. When Lyle dies, I'm going to haul him home to bury him. Personally, I wouldn't care if he was thrown over the nearest trash heap and left to the coyotes—there's no love lost between us—but I know Pa wants his only son planted back at the ranch."

Longarm studied the girl standing there beside Ma holding the cat. Finally, he shook his head, slipped past them, and scooped up the girl's gun from the hall floor. He handed the old Remington to her, butt-first. "You dropped somethin'."

"Thank you," Jenny said tonelessly, taking the gun.

"You always go around armed?"

"Yup."

Ma chuckled and smiled at Jenny.

Longarm found himself liking the girl. And he found himself believing her story, as well, though he was probably a fool for believing what anyone around here said. Regretfully, he said, "Hope I didn't hurt your hand."

"I'm pretty tough," the girl said. "It takes more than a little knock like that to hurt my hand."

Longarm pinched his hat brim to the pair. "Night, ladies."

"Marshal," Ma said and nodded as Longarm walked over to his own door, digging the key out of his pocket.

As he unlocked the door, he glanced over his shoulder at Jenny. She was looking at him over her own shoulder, but now she turned her head away quickly and stepped into her room. She bid Ma Marcus good night, let her eyes stray once more, furtively, to Longarm, then closed the door until the latch clicked.

Longarm went into his own room and tossed back a couple of stiff belts from Alva's good bourbon bottle before undressing and throwing himself under the blankets. His head was reeling. It didn't let him fall asleep until a good hour had passed.

Despite an unsatisfying night of sleep, Longarm woke at dawn as he usually did. He had a whore's bath, redressed his wounded right arm with the fixings Alva had provided, then left his room, wedging a matchstick between door and frame. As he headed down the stairs, he dug a three-for-a-nickel cheroot from his coat pocket, bit off the end, and struck a match on his cartridge belt.

Through the smoke billowing out around him, he saw Ma Marcus sweeping the lobby floor, dressed in another gaudy, high-necked dress that fit her spindly body like a second skin. This one was purple.

"You ever sleep, Ma?" he asked when he had the cigar going to his satisfaction, stepping down off the stairs.

"A few hours here and there." She stopped sweeping to regard him in her droll, matter-of-fact way. "I get occasional drummers coming in after midnight, and I ain't flush enough to turn 'em away. So I sit there with Sunshine"—she glanced at the Persian cat lying on a folded quilt atop the desk to Longarm's right—"and I crochet. Oh, well. What else am I gonna do? Too old to work the bawdy houses."

Longarm chuckled as he strolled past the good-humored old woman, heading for the doors.

"Almost forgot," she said. "Marshal Butter is in the dinin' room. Told me to send you in there."

"Thanks, Ma."

Longarm switched course and walked through the door flanking the lobby desk, into the dining room. Butter was the only customer, sitting where he and Longarm had supped the night before. The man looked weary, eyes red-rimmed, as he sagged back in a Windsor chair, a cup of coffee steaming in front of him, a brown-paper cigarette smoldering in his hand. His funnel-brimmed cream hat was on the table to his left.

"Mornin'," he said.

"Mornin' yourself," Longarm returned, doffing his hat and tossing it onto the table before him.

"What's your plan for the day?"

"I was going to check on Laughing Lyle," Longarm said. "And then I was going to backtrack him as far as the Finlay Roadhouse if need be, looking for those saddlebags."

"Ah, hell," Butter said, his voice gravelly from lack of sleep, looking up with his hound dog eyes. "Forget the damn saddlebags, Longarm. Ole Lyle hid 'em where no one's ever gonna find 'em, and he'll take the secret to his grave if he hasn't already."

"Just the same, I'm gonna take that ride."

Butter glanced at the serving girl standing off Longarm's right elbow, an expectant look in her eyes. She was the same girl from last night. There certainly must have been a paucity of sleep in Nowhere, Longarm vaguely reflected.

"Let's have some breakfast," Butter suggested. "Then I'll ride along with you. Two sets of eyes are better than one."

Longarm supposed the man was right, though he'd have prefered riding alone. He had a lot to think through. Then again, he might learn something from Butter during the long ride east and back again. What that might be, he had no idea.

Longarm ordered coffee and a breakfast platter, and when the girl hustled off to the kitchen, he sat down across from Butter. The girl brought his coffee a moment later, and only a few minutes after that, she brought both men large, oval plates heaped with ham and eggs, hash browns, and toast slathered in butter.

Butter had been oddly quiet, but now, as he ate, he looked across the table at Longarm and said with a faintly chagrined air, "I suppose you know where I headed off to last night. Oh, I don't reckon Benji would have told you. The kid respects my privacy. But if you'd talked to anyone else, they probably told you about my doin's up north of town . . . with Hetta."

"I'd be a liar if I said I hadn't heard," Longarm said over the rim of his coffee cup. "Don't worry about it, Roscoe. I sure as hell ain't. The way I see it, most men would have left the woman and the child high and dry. You didn't. I'd be proud of that fact, if I were you."

They ate for a time, and then Butter chuckled wryly and shook his head. "Never did get married. Never cared to. Preferred my freedom. I spent my whole life out on the range punchin' cows. Then, when I finally moved into town at age fifty-three and got myself a relatively secure job, what do I do? I throw a loop around a whole passel of trouble."

"Maybe you needed a family." Longarm had infrequently wondered about that himself, in the depths of deep, dark nights when he was alone and in a nowhere place such as this. "Well, now you have two."

"Ah, don't get me wrong. I'm right fond of my own kid and even the other two. It's just hard juggling Etta an' the kids and, well, Evelyn. And it ain't easy providin' for all of them."

Longarm swabbed his plate with a wedge of toast, stuffed the toast in his mouth, and sat back in his chair, thoroughly sated. He swallowed, sipped his coffee, and set the empty cup down on the table. He looked at the sheriff, feeling closer to the man after hearing his troubles, though that didn't mean he necessarily trusted him.

Longarm said, "Roscoe, I've always said that a man that don't have some complications in his life don't really have a life. What do you say we go check on ole Laughing Lyle, see if he's still kickin'. Then we'll lift some trail dust, find them saddlebags, and relieve me of at least one of my complications. 'Cause I'll tell you one thing—right now, on this job, I got plenty to go around!"

Chapter 13

"How's the patient, Doc?" Longarm inquired of Doc Bell when, a few minutes after he and Butter had left the hotel, the doctor answered the knock on his office door.

Bell ran a napkin over his mustache-mantled mouth as he chewed. He had another napkin tucked under his double chins for a bib. "Well, he's still kickin'," Bell said, glancing over his shoulder at Laughing Lyle's closed door. "But just barely. I got a feelin' he won't make it till lunch."

"That's what you said yesterday about supper."

"Well, Marshal, it's hard to predict these things," Bell said, sounding testy. "All I can tell you is what I told you yesterday—your bullets chewed up his insides pretty good. While I got the lead out of him, he's lost a lot of blood, and the internal damage is severe. If he ever leaves that room, I'll be very surprised."

Longarm stepped forward. "Let me get a look at him."

Bell didn't move but kept his large, sloppy bulk filling the half-open doorway, as though he was reluctant to let the lawman in. Longarm frowned at the man curiously.

Bell stepped back and drew the door wide. "All right, all right," he said, again sounding testy. "But he needs his sleep. If you're ever to take him back to Denver, you're gonna have to give him time to heal."

"If he's gonna die, anyway," Longarm said, "I reckon he'll be getting plenty of sleep soon enough."

He walked across the doctor's small office and pushed Laughing Lyle's door open, Butter and the doctor flanking him. He moved on into the room and stared down at the man, who looked about the same as he had before, breath raking loudly in and out of his lungs. Laughing Lyle's eyes were squeezed shut, and he had an anguished look on his face.

Longarm glanced at the small table beside the bed. There was a plate of fried eggs, bacon, and toast on it, as well as a half-drunk cup of coffee and a half-smoked cigarette. Longarm swung toward the door where Butter and Doc Bell stood, staring in at him.

"Whose breakfast?"

"Mine," Doc Bell said, hiking a shoulder. "I was keeping watch on him. He'd started coughing earlier, and I thought he might have fluid in his lungs." He shrugged again, slapped a hand to his thigh. "I did take the Hippocratic oath, Marshal Long . . ."

Longarm looked down at Laughing Lyle once more. The wounded killer squeezed his eyes closed tighter, opened his thick lips, and made a gurgling sound deep in his throat. A muscle in his cheek twitched.

Longarm walked back to the door as the two other men stepped away from it, the doctor backing toward his desk. "Keep him alive, Doc. Remember that oath."

Doc Bell threw up his hands. "I'm doing everything I can, Marshal. Everything I can . . ."

"If he's havin' trouble breathing, it might help if you don't smoke in his room," Longarm said. "I'll stop back later."

"See you, Doc," Butter said, donning his hat and following Longarm out of the office. As both men strode west, Butter said, "Well, he don't look good, but at least he's still kickin'. Any chance we could try him and hang him here?"

"Don't I wish, Roscoe," Longarm said. "Don't I wish."

Longarm and Butter retrieved their mounts from Humperdink's rear paddock and saddled the mounts themselves as Humperdink worked on another coffin—this one for the wolfer, Dave Ross, who was laid out on planks stretched across a pair of sawhorses just inside the double front doors. The dead man's long, gray hair blew around in the morning breeze as Longarm and Butter walked their mounts out the barn's double doors and into the street.

"If you're off to fetch me some more business, Marshal," Humperdink said with a wink and a grin, "I sure do appreciate it! I could eat a T-bone every night of the week!" He laughed.

"Shut up, A.J.," Butter admonished. "You just con-

centrate on gettin' ole Dave in the ground before he
starts stinkin' up the place!"

Longarm gave a wry snort as he turned the smoky
gray around, grinding his heels into the gelding's flanks.
He and Butter galloped eastward along the broad main
street still filled with charcoal shadows, as the sun was
only just now peeking above the eastern horizon.

They rode hard for a time, then walked their horses,
knowing they could have a long ride ahead of them and
wanting to save the beasts. Around nine o'clock, Longarm shed his buckskin mackinaw, for the sun was well
up and turning the day warm. They didn't pay much
attention to the trail for the first hour's ride, because
Bethany and her father, Reverend Todd, had come upon
Laughing Lyle farther east. It was after leaving there that
Longarm would begin scouring the trail again for any
sign of the outlaw having left it to hide the saddlebags.

Probably, Laughing Lyle had known he was running
out of steam shortly before he'd finally passed out from
blood loss and exhaustion, and had hidden the saddlebags only a mile or so east of where he'd finally col-
lapsed. At least, that's what Longarm hoped. Otherwise,
he and Butter might have to backtrack all the way to
Finlay's. The federal lawman certainly wouldn't mind
seeing the lovely Alva again, but he had to keep his nose
to the grindstone, so to speak.

The last thing he wanted to do was return empty-
handed to Denver. Getting the saddlebags back to Stoneville was first and foremost on his mind. Bringing
Laughing Lyle to justice was second. However, another
night with Alva or the lovely Bethany was a close third.

A little after ten, he and Butter approached the place

where Longarm had seen the marks in the trail where the Reverend Todd and Bethany had picked up Laughing Lyle. He and Butter spooked a couple of coyotes that had been hunting in the brush on the trail's north side. The brush wolves went loping off to the west and north, one glancing indignantly back over its shoulder. Longarm drew rein and stared down at the marks in the trail, which had faded considerably over the past day or so but were still visible.

"This is the place, eh?" Butter said.

"Yep." Longarm started to boot his gray along the trail, but then he turned his attention back to something he'd spied on the ground near where Laughing Lyle had lain unconscious.

"What is it?" Butter said.

Longarm swung down from his saddle and, holding onto the gray's reins, knelt beside a large brown splotch near where the trail from the north entered the main one. Longarm removed his right-hand glove and touched two fingers to the splotch, rubbing the dirt around between them.

"Blood?" Butter asked.

Longarm nodded.

"Well, the doc said ole Lyle lost a barrelful."

"Yeah, but this blood here is a good three feet from where Laughing Lyle fell in the trail." Longarm pointed at the bloodstain marking where a body had lain. "See there? How could more of *his* blood get this far over *here*? I mean, the man couldn't have been *spewin'* the stuff or he'd be dead by now for certain-sure."

"What the hell you think it's from, then?" Butter said from his saddle.

Remembering the two coyotes, Longarm looked into the brush and rocks inside the pie-shaped wedge of ground where the two trails came together. Glancing back along the trail, he spied two broad furrows to his right. They angled off the trail and into the brush.

Frowning curiously, silently admonishing himself for not having noticed the tracks the day before, he walked through the brush, following the two furrows. Crusty brown blood drops spotted the brush on either side of him, and on several rocks, as well. Ahead lay a low, natural embankment. The furrows rose up the embankment, as did Longarm.

He gazed down the other side and drew a breath.

He let it out in a surprised whistle as he studied the dead man before him, lying back down and parallel to the bank. He was a tall, slender, severe-looking man with a thin salt-and-pepper mustache and even thinner salt-and-pepper hair. He wore black wool trousers, a black coat over a black clergy vest, and a clerical collar. Thick blood had crusted around a large hole in his chest—an instantly killing shot through the heart.

Whoever had shot him from point-blank range and rolled him down the bank had seen fit to cross his powdery white hands on his flat belly, however. Good of 'em, Longarm thought. Damn nice.

"Holy shit!" exclaimed Roscoe Butter, who had followed Longarm and now stood beside him atop the bank. "That's Reverend Todd!"

"Had a feelin' it might be." Longarm glanced at Todd and ran a hand across the back of his neck, wincing at the growing perplexity of his visit to Nowhere. "I thought you said the good reverend and his charming daughter had hauled Laughing Lyle to town?"

Butter turned his shocked, rheumy brown gaze to Longarm. "I thought they did! Or, at least, I *figured* they did. I never saw the reverend myself. Only the girl."

Butter swabbed his forehead with a handkerchief, looking perplexed, then snapped his fingers together loudly. "Come to think of it, she mentioned somethin' about her father trampin' off home before I got there, as he'd caught a chill during their ride and thought he might be comin' down with somethin'!"

Longarm's ears began ringing in shame and confusion. He'd let the little bitch hoodwink him into believing she was nothing more than an innocent, frustrated girl hemmed in by her remote environs as well as her preacher father. But there was nothing innocent about Miss Todd. No, sir. Somehow, she'd aligned herself with Laughing Lyle his own self, and either she or Laughing Lyle had shot the reverend right here where he and his daughter had come upon the killer passed out on the trail.

How that had come to pass, Longarm had no idea. And he still had no idea where the saddlebags were, but something told him now, in light of Reverend Todd's murder, that the saddlebags were a whole lot closer to Nowhere than he'd at first thought. In fact, they could have been under the bed that he in his idiocy had allowed Bethany to lead him to and in which he had in fact fucked her!

"Roscoe," Longarm said, ears burning as he turned and began tramping back toward the horses, "I do believe we'd best hightail it back to Nowhere."

Butter jogged, breathing hard, to keep up. "What're you thinkin', Longarm? You think Laughing Lyle killed the reverend *in front of his own daughter?*"

"Either that or, seeing the saddlebags and knowin' her pa would have none of the stolen loot, she killed him herself."

"Holy shit!"

"That's likely what the reverend said." Longarm grabbed his gray's reins and toed a stirrup. "Appropriate last words, given the circumstances."

As Butter swung into his own saddle, the older lawman said, "Don't you think we'd best haul the reverend back to town?"

"We'll send Benji for him with a buckboard. I want to get back to Nowhere pronto. Miss Todd has some very pertinent questions to answer!"

As Longarm rammed the heels of his cavalry stovepipes against the smoky gray's flanks, Butter gave a grunt behind him. The grunt had not yet died on the town marshal's lips when a rifle's shrieking report reached Longarm's ears. Smoke puffed south of the main trail, from atop a long, low hill spotted with clay-colored rocks, rabbit brush, and piñon pines.

Longarm glanced behind and to his left to see Butter grabbing his upper left arm and pulling back on his claybank's reins with the opposite hand. At the same time, the horse reared, screaming shrilly. As Butter yelled and tumbled out of the saddle over his horse's left hip, Longarm checked his own horse down while reaching for his Winchester.

Smoke puffed again on the top of the low ridge, and the bullet screeched passed Longarm's left ear as he slid the Winchester from its saddle sheath. Another slug seared a hot line across the outside of his right knee, tearing his pants. His horse reared just as Butter's had done and just as he'd grabbed his rifle, finding him unprepared.

He lost hold of the reins, tumbled backward, and rolled off the horse's hindquarters, the ground coming up hard to ram against the back of his head and shoulders as another bullet plowed into the trail about six inches to his right, blowing sand and gravel in his face.

"Holy *shit!*" he heard Butter intone as the town marshal's horse gave another shrill scream and fell in a heap beside him.

Chapter 14

As his horse galloped off up the trail, Longarm saw his rifle lying in the brush. He pushed off his elbows and heels and dashed toward it, but when he was two feet away, the rifle on the ridgetop thundered twice more, and two slugs hammered the trail in front of Longarm's own Winchester.

He cursed as he threw himself behind a rock. Climbing to his knees and spitting grit from his lips and mustache, he glanced at Butter.

The marshal lay on his back, clutching his left arm with his right hand and groaning, breathing hard. His horse had fallen on his left leg. He tugged on it, trying to tug it free, but there was no doing. Blood dribbled from the horse's left eye as it lay on Butter as though it had fallen from the sky.

The town marshal was a sitting duck, so Longarm took advantage of a lull in the shooter's firing. He leaped over his covering rock, grabbed his rifle, and racked a round into the breech. Snugging the Winchester's brass butt plate to his right shoulder, he aimed at the tan hat crown he could see rising just above the ridge, and the bristling rifle barrel.

He fired three rounds, watching his slugs blow up dust near the hat and rifle. One spanged off a rock to the shooter's left. He thought he saw the hat jerk, as though the ricochet might have clipped the dry-gulcher.

Then the hat and rifle disappeared behind the ridge, and Longarm ran over to Butter.

"How bad you hit, Roscoe?"

"Not bad, but galdangit, I can't pull my leg free from beneath my damn hoss!"

Longarm glanced once more at the ridge. The hat and the rifle barrel were there again, the rifle leveling on him and Butter. A chill raked Longarm. He shouted, "Hold on!" and, on one knee, fired two shots again quickly toward the shooter. The dry-gulcher's own rifle stabbed smoke and flames, and the slug plowed into the back of the already dead horse, causing it to jerk a little.

Longarm fired again, until his Winchester's hammer pinged on an empty chamber. Then he tossed the long gun aside and, keeping one eye on the ridge, positioned himself behind Butter, snaked his arms under the town marshal's, and pulled. Butter groaned, throwing his head back painfully, gritting his teeth. On Longarm's second hard yank, Butter's leg came free.

"God*damn*!" yelled the town marshal.

"You got a blue tongue—anyone ever tell you that, Roscoe?"

"Also got a goddamn twisted ankle!"

Longarm dragged the man into the brush on the far

side of the trail from the shooter, then ran back to the town marshal's horse and slid his Spencer repeater from the saddle boot. "Gonna borrow this for a minute, Roscoe!" he said, working the rifle's trigger guard cocking lever to rack a live cartridge into the breech.

Longarm leaped over the dead horse just as another slug plowed into the trail nearby, followed a quarter second later by the angry bellow of the shooter's rifle. Longarm ran into the rocks and shrubs, heading toward the ridge and thinking that the ambusher had more determination than talent.

Two slugs plowed up sand and grass on each side of him, and then he dropped to a knee, aimed the Spencher, and fired.

The rifle leaped and roared, smacking his shoulder. The slug loudly hammered the rock to the shooter's left. Longarm fired again and then, not seeing the tan hat or the rifle, took off running toward the ridge, pumping his arms and legs, carrying the rifle in one hand. He jerked his gaze back and forth from the terrain in front of him to the top of the ridge, and then, not seeing the tan hat, he ran up the hill.

It was low but steep. By the time he was halfway to the top, Longarm was breathing hard, the taste of copper in his mouth, and silently cursing his three-for-a-nickel cheroot habit.

Six feet from the top, he slowed his pace and aimed the rifle straight out from his shoulder. Two more steps and he could see the gap in the rocks from which the shooter had fired on him and Butter. All that was there now was a slight indentation of an elbow and a knee, and ten or so brass cartridge casings.

Hooves thudded.

Longarm lifted his gaze to see a horseback rider galloping up the next ridge beyond him. The shooter was
too far away for Longarm to make out many details
except the tan hat and a black vest over a blue shirt.
Saddlebags flapped across the long-legged, white-
stockinged, calico horse's hindquarters.

Longarm dropped to a knee, but just as he got the
Spencer aimed, the shooter plunged over the top of the
opposite ridge and disappeared down the other side. The
hoof thuds dwindled quickly.

Longarm lowered the rifle, raking air in and out of
his lungs and off-cocking the Spencer's hammer. He
stared after the fled shooter. Who the hell was he? Just
one more of Dave Ross's ilk, out to drill him for the same
reason that Ross likely had? Or maybe someone Bethany
Todd has sent.

He wondered if the saddlebags the dry-gulcher was
packing were the ones containing the Stoneville loot.

Damn puzzling.

Ignoring his previous self-scolding, Longarm dug a
cheroot from his coat pocket as he gained his feet, turned,
and started back down the hill. He fired a lucifer to life
on his holster, touched the flame to the cigar, and had it
going to his satisfaction as he gained the hill's bottom
and was tramping back toward the trail.

Ahead, Butter sat on a rock, extending his left leg
and leaning forward with his right hand on that thigh.
He'd knotted his neckerchief around the opposite arm.
His hat was off and his teeth shone between spread lips
as he stared across his dead horse at Longarm.

"You get that son of a bitch?" he asked as Longarm stepped onto the trail.

The federal lawman shook his head. "No, but we'll see him again. How's your leg?"

"Just twisted. I'll live."

"Too bad about your horse."

"Yeah, he was a good horse."

Longarm hated to see animals killed for no reason. Just as frustrating was the fact that he and Butter would now have to ride double on their return to Nowhere, which meant that if they didn't want to kill the gray, they'd have to take it slow. It would probably take them twice as long getting back as it had coming.

And that meant there was no way in hell they'd be able to catch up to the horse-killing dry-gulcher, though he'd been headed back in the direction of town.

Longarm puffed his cigar as he found his hat and loaded his rifle. He set the long gun on his shoulder and headed off in search of his horse. He found it cropping bunchgrass a quarter-mile north of the trail, his McClellan saddle hanging down its side.

He reset the saddle and blanket and inspected the horse for wounds and grazes; pried a stone out from beneath its right front shoe with his pocketknife, then deemed the animal sound and rode it back to where Butter was smoking a cigarette, where Longarm had left him.

"Hate to leave my saddle," the town marshal said, looking down at his horse as he limped toward the gray.

"Benji'll fetch it for you when he fetches the preacher."

"That saddle's about all I own that's worth anything—that, my six-gun, and the old Spencer."

Longarm helped the older man onto the gray behind him, then, cursing under his breath in frustration once more at the long, slow trip they had ahead of them, he booted the horse forward at a fast walk.

It was nearly dusk when Longarm topped a rise and saw Nowhere spread out before him, slanting down the bench aproning out from the southernmost ridge of the Organ Range. The sun was about halfway down on the settlement's far side, and shadows angled out from the buildings lining both sides of the street.

As Longarm gigged the tired gelding forward, he looked around carefully, half-expecting, as he'd half-expected all the way back to town, for the bushwhacker to show himself again. Darkening alley mouths would be a good place to affect another ambush, as would a second- or third-story window.

"What the hell?" Butter said, riding behind him and pointing straight ahead toward Humperdink's livery barn on the far side of the town. The barn's double doors were open wide, and a lighted lantern glowed inside, half-silhouetting the big, burly, overall-clad frame of the liveryman/coroner. "Looks like A.J.'s workin' overtime. That ain't like him. He usually kicks off around three and heads over to the Nowhere for beer and a free sandwich."

Longarm shuttled his gaze from the jostling figure of Humperdink apparently nailing another coffin together, to the Nowhere Saloon. Tension emanated from the half dozen men milling outside the place, smoking and drinking and speaking in hushed tones, glancing up the street and toward its other side. The horses tied to the hitch racks fronting the saloon seemed to sense the men's anxiety, for they fidgeted around, switching their tails and tossing their heads.

A big man with a heavy-footed gait was walking toward the saloon from the direction of the doctor's office. Just as Longarm was about to rein up in front of the Nowhere and ask what all the commotion was about, the big man came running with surprising speed until Longarm saw Benji's broad, fleshy face beneath the narrow brim of the shabby bowler hat. The hat nearly blew off the big deputy town marshal's head before he could grab it and hold it in one fist as he ran.

"Marshal Butter," the kid cried, breathing hard, his face pinched with anguish. "Somethin' just *awful* happened!"

Longarm knew right away it had to do with Laughing Lyle. Before Benji could reach him and Butter, Longarm rammed his boot heels into the gray's flanks, and the poor, tired creature lunged forward and sort of shambled past the big deputy to Doc Bell's two-story, adobe-brick office.

"Hey!" Benji cried, wheeling and running back toward the office.

"Oh, no," Butter said. "Oh, good Lord—don't tell me . . . !"

Longarm had barely stopped the horse before he lifted his right leg over the animal's neck and dropped straight down to the ground. He pulled his Colt from its holster and bounded over the roofed boardwalk and through the doctor's front door. He stopped just inside and lowered the pistol.

It was not Laughing Lyle he saw in the room Long-

arm had last seen him in, but Ma Marcus from the
Organ Range House. She was tending a man laid out on
the bed. The man was too big to be Laughing Lyle.

There was a thud to Longarm's left, and he turned to
arch a surprised brow at Laughing Lyle's half sister,
Jenny May, who, regarding him obliquely, dropped a
chunk of wood into the potbelly stove that stood in the
middle of the room, beside a leather-padded operating
table. A pan of water steamed on the stove. Jenny turned
her eyes away from Longarm, vaguely sheepish, as Ma
Marcus turned toward the federal lawman and said in a
scolding tone, "About time you got here."

Butter limped up onto the boardwalk behind Longarm, flanked by the anguished-looking Benji, and
stepped inside. "What the hell happened, Ma?"

"And you!" Ma scolded, wagging a finger at the town
marshal. "No offense to Benji, but where in the hell have
you been all day? Last I heard you were still the law of
this little backwater!"

In four long strides, Longarm was in the room with
Ma Marcus and looking down at the writhing, groaning
form of Doc Bell himself, fully clothed but covered with
a bloody sheet. Only his face was visible. Bell's eyes
were squeezed shut and beads of perspiration stood out
across his pale forehead.

As Butter limped into the room behind him, Longarm
drew the sheet down from the doctor's neck. He winced
when he saw the blood-matted bandage that apparently
Ma Marcus had applied to his belly, about halfway
between the man's belly button and his heart.

"It was Laughing Lyle!" cried Benji, stumbling in
behind the town marshal. "He shot the doc and the doc's

wife—damn near blew Mrs. Bell in two!—and then him and that girl took off on horseback, galloping toward the Organ Range!"

"And Laughing as he did it, too," said Ma, shaking her head in the doorway, holding a wadded up rag in one withered hand. "Whoopin' and hollerin', him and the preacher's girl triggerin' shots all over town, and then ole Lyle galloped north toward the mountains, Laughing like he was just havin' the time of his life!"

"The girl?" Longarm said, swinging his gaze toward the spindly hotel owner standing in the doorway. "You mean Bethany Todd?"

"I sure do!"

"Was she riding a calico?"

"She was indeed."

"Did she have a pair of bulging saddlebags on her?"

"Shore 'nuff!" intoned Benji, beating Ma to the punch.

Ma laughed without mirth, as though at the sickest, darkest joke she'd ever heard. "I knew somethin' was up around here. I just had a feelin'. Call it my sixth sense. But who would ever suspect it—eh, Marshal? The preacher's daughter runnin' off her leash with Laughing Lyle May!"

Chapter 15

"Miss Bethany?" Butter said, aghast, standing there at the end of Doc Bell's bed, leaning on his Spencer rifle. "Why, she musta shot her poor pa, then . . ." He let his voice trail off as though it were all just too much to fathom. His face was sweat-shiny and white.

The preacher's daughter killing her father and throwing in with Laughing Lyle . . .

Longarm himself still hadn't wrapped his own mind around the entire sordid thing, but he knew now it was Bethany who'd ambushed him and Todd. She'd probably gone out to retrieve the saddlebags from wherever she'd stowed them along the trail the night she'd found the wounded Laughing Lyle and her father, and had seen Longarm and Butter riding out from Nowhere. She'd probably figured they'd find the reverend's body, so she followed them and tried to beef them both when it seemed convenient, in hopes of saving her and Laughing Lyle from having to do it later. Or being prevented from getting out of town.

The girl wasn't half-bad with a rifle. Almost too good.

Longarm moved now to Ma Marcus, who was flanked by both Benji and Laughing Lyle's half sister, Jenny.

"Ma, where did Bethany come from? Did she ride into town from the east a couple of hours ago?"

"I don't know where she come from," Ma said in her gravelly voice. "I just know I heard gunfire and the doctor yellin' and his wife screamin' and Laughing Lyle whoopin' and hollerin', and I ran out of the hotel to see her, Miss Bethany, sitting her calico in front of the place. She had the reins of another saddled horse in her hand, and she threw the reins to Lyle as he came limpin' out of the doctor's office. Before he mounted up, he swung around and fired two more shots into the office."

Benji yelled, "Ain't that some way to treat a man who saved your life?"

"He's gotta be a devil," Butter said, staring at Longarm. "To do that, shot up as bad as he was."

"Are you sure he was shot up as bad as you thought?" Longarm asked the town marshal.

"Well, yeah . . . of course." Butter slid his stricken gaze toward the writhing Doc Bell. "You heard the doc. Said your bullets tore him all up inside."

Benji gave a yelp, like a coyote peppered with buckshot, and went running out of the office, his heavy hoof thuds rocking the entire building. He whipped past the window and was gone.

Longarm returned his gaze to Butter. The town marshal looked away. Longarm walked back over to the side of the bed and stared down at Bell. The doctor's eyes were open, haunting in their directness.

He stretched his lips back from his teeth as though in agony then lifted his head, grunting and muttering. He lifted his hand, weakly wagging his fingers. He seemed to be trying to say something.

"What is it, Doc?" Longarm crouched low and squeezed the dying man's shoulder. "What do you want to tell me?"

Doc Bell stared at Longarm, gritting his teeth, sweat oozing in several rivulets down his cheeks. He grabbed Longarm's forearm and squeezed, stretched his lips back farther, gurgling, saliva bubbling between his teeth.

"What is it, Doc?" Longarm said. "What're you tryin' to tell me, goddamnit?"

Bell's grip on Longarm's forearm loosened. The hand dropped away. The man's eyes fluttered closed and his head sagged back against his pillow. His breath rattled, and his chest and belly fell still.

"Dead," Butter said. "How do you like that?"

Longarm looked at the town marshal, who shook his head, holding his hat down low by his side as he leaned against his rifle. Did he really appear relieved or was it just Longarm's fevered imagination?

How much, if anything, did Butter know about Laughing Lyle's ploy?

"Poor man," Ma said, shaking her head slowly before turning to Jenny. "There's no need for the water, I guess, dear. Thank you for helping."

Longarm looked beyond the woman at Jenny, who

stood holding the tin pan of steaming water. The girl stared back at Longarm, but it was as though she were staring right through him, shaking her head.

"What is it, Miss May?"

Her vision suddenly cleared. She flushed slightly, frowning. "What? I . . . was . . . just thinking what a horror my brother is, of course." She glanced at the dead doctor. "More blood on the May name."

Her eyes glazed with tears, and her upper lip quivered. Ma went to her, wrapped an arm around the girl's shoulders. "We can't pick our own kin, child."

Longarm stood before Jenny, gently took the steaming pan of water from her, and set it on the doctor's desk. He turned back to the girl, frowning down at her. "Do you know where's he's headed? Your ranch, maybe?"

Jenny gasped. Her dark eyes acquired a sudden, stricken cast. "Lyle might head there for fresh horses. If so, my father is there alone. There'll be trouble."

"How so?"

"They don't get along, and with Pa drinkin' the way he does . . ."

The girl ran her hands back through her hair and stared at the floor, eyes wide with worry. "The problem, you see, is they're cut from the same cloth." She shook her head. "I should have ridden after them right away, but I wanted to help Ma with the doctor. Oh, God!" She sobbed, tears, dribbling down her cheeks.

Longarm glanced at Ma. "Best help get her back to her room." As the old woman turned Jenny around and walked her toward the door, Longarm turned to Butter. "You know the way out to the May ranch?"

"Of course."

"Well, follow me over to the livery barn and tell me while I saddle a fresh horse."

"You ain't goin' after 'em in the dark, are ya, Longarm?"

Longarm headed out the door. "I sure as hell am."

He'd been after those saddlebags too long and hard to let a little darkness stop him now. And Bethany Todd had played him for a fool. Besides, there would be a moon tonight. That should help keep him from killing his horse.

Butter said, "Well, I'll go with you, for chrissakes."

"No, you stay here in case they circle back."

Longarm didn't figure Laughing Lyle would do that. The real reason he didn't want Butter riding with him was because he wasn't sure he trusted the man, not to mention he was injured. Laughing Lyle's sudden recovery had thrown Butter and Bell under a heavy blanket of suspicion in the federal lawman's eyes.

As he led the horse over to the livery barn, Butter hobbled along behind him, warning him about all the hidden dangers in that mountainous terrain north of town. But Longarm was only half-listening. His ears were burning over Bethany Todd. He could still see those breasts in the darkness, feel those delicious lips on his, her sleek snatch grinding against his throbbing hard-on.

All the time they'd frolicked she'd likely snickered to herself over the ruse she'd pulled, her father turning cold on the trail east of Nowhere. Maybe Laughing Lyle was a devil. But he'd teamed up with a girl just as devilish, though you sure as hell wouldn't know it to look at her. Or to fuck her!

"If that ain't enough business for you, Doc Bell will

be here shortly," Longarm told Humperdink as he
glanced at the body of the middle-aged, portly woman,
Doc's wife, stretched out on sawhorses just inside the
barn's double doors. She was only partly covered by a
sheet, and Longarm saw a mess of blood matting her
flowered dress. Her puffy, pale face and curly gray hair
were liberally splattered, as well. Her eyes were halfway
open, and her tongue drooped from one corner of her
mouth.

"Jeepers!" Humperdink cried, looking up from the
casket he was hammering together and removing the
two nails he had clamped between his lips. "If I get any
more business, there ain't gonna be nothin' left of
Nowhere! You goin' after him, Marshal?"

"What do you think?"

Longarm had stopped the gray just outside the barn's
double doors and was unbuckling the McClellan's belly
strap. "I guess you didn't actually see the preacher the
other night, did you? In the buggy with Bethany and
Laughing Lyle?"

"No, I was in back sleepin', as I tend to do that hour
of the night." Humperdink snorted sheepishly and hiked
his blue coveralls higher across his sagging belly. "But
when I got out here, she said he was feelin' poorly and
had tramped on home."

"You didn't think that sounded funny—the reverend
leaving his daughter here with Laughing Lyle?"

Humperdink looked around uncertainly, shrugging
his heavy shoulders. "Well, I don't know. I was half-
asleep! But I called for Marshal Butter pronto." He
glanced at Longarm as the federal lawman carried his

saddle and blanket past him into the barn. "Say, what's this about? The reverend's all right, ain't he?"

"Forget it," Longarm said, dropping the saddle over a buggy wheel and heading for the rear paddock. "I need a good horse, Humperdink. Come on back here and point out your best one for hard and fast mountain travel!"

For two hours, Longarm pushed the fleet-footed, wide-barreled buckskin as hard as he dared. The three-quarter moon kited high over the jagged, black-velvet ridges in the southwest, fairly well lighting the narrow horse trail he climbed into the perilous reaches of the Organ Range.

For most of those two hours he'd ridden up and over the rock-strewn hogbacks that rolled down from the severe southern ridge like frozen ocean swells. But now, following the trail up a canyon that twisted higher into the mountains, the going was more treacherous. At times, the moon was hidden by towering crags, and he had to walk the horse. In a few cases, he slipped down out of the saddle and led the mount by its reins, not wanting it to kick a rock and lose a shoe or tumble down a boulder-strewn crevasse.

Occasionally, when the moon lit the trail, he spied a print left by a recent horse, and he knew that he was on the right path. As far as he could tell, there was no one else out here, and all the inhabitants of these remote reaches were likely holed up in ranch cabins or huddled around fires in dark canyons. The print had to belong to Laughing Lyle or Bethany's horse.

Finally, when he'd ridden for three hours, he realized

it was time for him to make camp. He'd come to where
several trails branched off the main one, and he couldn't
remember which one Butter had told him led to the May
ranch. Slide rock littered the trails, making it impossible
to tell if any horses had recently passed.

Grumbling to himself, wanting desperately to have
caught up to Laughing Lyle and that killing bitch of his
before they reached the May ranch, Longarm led the
buckskin down off the main trail through piñons and
balsam pines. A creek ran through the bottom of this
gorge, nestled between bulging granite walls and steep,
forested slopes sparsely tufted with brush. The ridges
vaulted around Longarm, two or three thousand feet high
in some places. He could see a few stars between the
stygian peaks, but the moon had sunk behind a particularly large stone pinnacle.

It was cold at night this far above sea level. Longarm
could see his and his horse's breath. When he'd tended
the animal and tied him to a short picket line between
trees, he donned his mackinaw, which he'd carried over
his hotroll, and tramped around the shore of the gurgling creek, gathering firewood.

He piled the small pine and fir sticks beside a hastily
prepared stone ring and touched a match to a tinder
mound of crushed pinecones and dead leaves. Gradually, he added more and larger branches to the growing
blaze. He'd need a good fire to keep the chill out of his
bones.

He filled his coffeepot at the creek, first taking a long
drink of the toothachingly cold water. When he'd set
the coffeepot in the fire, he fished around in his saddlebags but found only a few bits of old jerky and stony

hardtack. Sitting against a tree bole, he poked up his hat brim and lifted his eyes to the nearby creek flashing red in the light of his fire.

There might be fish in there. And he had nothing else to do while his coffee boiled . . .

He took his small canvas sewing kit out of his saddle-bags, removed the fishhook pinned inside of it, and produced a small roll of fishing line from a side pouch. Finding a nice-sized worm under a rock, he impaled the bait on the hook and tied a .44 cartridge just above the hook for weight and reflection. He knelt down beside the stream and dropped the hook in the water.

To his surprise, in less than two minutes, there was a tug on the line, and he pulled in the wriggling red-throated trout that was about eight inches long and packing just enough meat to keep him from going to bed hungry.

Longarm felt better about everything now, occupied with gutting the fish and roasting it on a stick over the fire while he sipped his piping black Arbuckles. The only thing missing was a shot of Maryland rye. He'd left Alva's bourbon back in his room at the Organ Range House.

He'd just finished the deliciously fresh and tender fish when he noticed that the coyotes that had been yammering from one ridge and the lone wolf that had been crying from another ridge had suddenly fallen silent. There was only the breathy snapping of his fire, the frequent pop of pine resin.

Somewhere back in the direction from which he'd come, a horse whinnied. The sound was muffled by distance and by jutting ridges rising between him and the horse.

Longarm jerked with a start when his own horse lifted an answering whinny from just behind him. He jerked again when another horse, not far beyond the far side of the stream, also loosed a shrill reply. Hooves clacked on rock.

"Hallooo the fire!" a man's voice called. "Don't get touchy or nothin', fella. We're friendly!"

Chapter 16

Longarm knew they weren't friendly.

If they were friendly, they wouldn't be out tramping around the Organ Range in the middle of the night. Unless they were lawmen like him, of course. Or cowpunchers.

But he hadn't seen any cows, and he doubted there were any other lawmen as foolish as he was to be stalking badmen alone out here. He'd known badge-toters who'd tracked owlhoots on this backside of the devil's ass, and they'd always told him with a sharp glint in their eyes that the Organs were no place for a lawman to venture without a sizable, gun-savvy posse.

"Ain't that a coincidence," he called, grabbing his rifle and stepping wide of the fire. "I'm friendly, too. Ride in slow and keep your hands where I can see 'em till we get to know each other."

On the far side of the narrow brook, shadows jostled. Hooves clacked on stones, brush crackled, and tack squawked. Longarm could see the occasional flash of silver saddle trimmings and what was most likely gun steel. There must have been a trail down the opposite canyon wall that he hadn't seen in the darkness, because the shadows seemed to materialize out of the darkness over there and somewhere above.

Then the lead rider drew rein on the far side of the stream. Two more came up to stop slightly behind him. Longarm couldn't tell much about them except that they wore battered hats and chaps and one man had his chaps decked out with silver conchos. He had them on his shell belt, too. Rifles jutted from saddle boots.

"Seen your fire," said the lead man, his face dark beneath his hat brim. "Figured we might as well pull in. We got grub enough to share."

"Already ate," Longarm said. "But you're welcome to the fire. Come on over."

He'd have preferred to bivouac alone, but now that they were here, he had little choice but to invite them into his camp. If he sent them on, they might take offense and try to pink him from the darkness.

"You're not Shanley, are ya?" asked the lead rider as he booted his white-socked black horse across the creek. The others eased their own mounts down the opposite bank and came across, too, water splashing, the horse snorting.

"Nope," Longarm said. "I ain't Shanley."

"Figured you weren't," said the lead rider as his horse lunged up the near bank and stopped, giving its head a fierce toss. "We're supposed to meet a man named Shanley. Been lookin' for him three nights in a row."

"That's enough, Jake," said the man stopping his

zebra dun off the lead rider's right stirrup. "Don't be so goddamned chatty. Can't you see you're borin' him."

Jake chuckled and shook his head. He was short and stocky, with a sandy spade beard jutting off his chin. "That's me—a real gasser. Out here, you get that way . . . if you're out here long enough. Everything's so damn quiet, you wanna talk and talk!" He chuckled again.

The dark, mustached man to his right said, "Mind if we picket our hosses with yours, mister?"

"As long as they're friendly." Uneasily, Longarm sat down against the tree. His rifle was leaning against the tree on his right, within easy reach if he needed it.

"Obliged," said Jake, swinging down from his saddle. The all led their horses off toward where the buckskin nickered curiously, cautiously, shuffling around and snorting.

Longarm sipped his coffee, keeping the three strangers in the corner of his right eye as they unsaddled and rubbed down their horses. When they were finished, they came over grunting and toting their saddles and bedrolls, their rifle scabbards still attached to the saddles. They plopped their gear down around the fire, one to each side of Longarm, and Jake on the fire's far side. The air around the camp was rife now with the smell of horse and man sweat and pine and the fish Longarm had roasted over the fire.

The man to his left was tall, lanky, and dark, while the man to his right was of medium height and long-haired, with a stiff, brushy mustache curving down over his mouth. He kept his eyes off Longarm. Jake chuckled in a habitually nervous, affable way, letting his own quick eyes dart across the fire at the lawman. The tall, lanky man who appeared not yet twenty looked grim, insolent, brooding, perpetually angry.

Owlhoots, Longarm thought. On the dodge and looking for a man named Shanley to throw in with for another job, maybe. Or maybe Shanley would give them a place to hole up quietly until their dust settled and they could hightail it to Mexico with fresh horses.

"Coffee?" Longarm set his own cup down to keep one hand free, and used a leather swatch to hold up the coffeepot.

"Don't mind if we do," said Jake.

They already had their tin cups out, and they extended them around the fire to Longarm. He filled them using his left hand and keeping a mild expression on his face. When all the cups were filled, the strangers sat back and sipped the hot brew, as did Longarm.

No one said anything for a time, and then Jake said, "Sure is chilly. Me, I'll be happy to crawl into the ole hotroll tonight. Just wish I had a woman." He gave a soft whoop of anticipated glee. "Ain't had me one for a month of Sundays. Don't see many out here."

He looked at his friends as though expecting them to say something. The tall, brooding kid just stared into his cup as he drank it.

The dark man sat back against his saddle with one knee up. He had a pistol positioned over his belly, the handle jutting up toward his chest. Occasionally, he slid short, cunning glances toward Longarm. And then the brooding kid started glancing at him, too, and the cold, pointed nails of witches' fingers began tickling Longarm behind his ears.

He'd play a hunch.

"Yeah, not too many women out here," he said, blowing ripples on his coffee and sipping. "Especially not many like ole Laughing Lyle's gal, huh?"

Silence.

The three owlhoots looked at him. Jake still had that affable grin, but it was dwindling slowly, his blue eyes acquiring a faintly nervous edge.

"Uh . . . who's that?" he asked.

"You know—the hombre you ran into up the trail. The one with the pretty blonde. The one who offered you a sizable amount of cash to scour his backtrail for Deputy United States Marshal Custis Long." Longarm stared across the fire at Jake, but he could see the other two very clearly in the periphery of his vision. "Me."

A silence followed, so heavy that it was as if a twenty-ton boulder were suspended over the camp by a slender string. The fire popped and sparked.

The dark man to Longarm's left flicked his hand toward the handle of the hogleg over his belly. Longarm pulled his Frontier Colt from its cross-draw holster and shot the dark man just as he clicked his pistol's hammer back.

At the same time, Jake gave a yell and clawed for his own two six-shooters, but the kid to Longarm's right was a hair faster, so Longarm shot him next. And then, just as Jake's own pistols roared, Jake was punched straight back by the .44 slug that Longarm had, an eye wink before, sent hurling toward his chest, to tear his heart in two before ricocheting off his spine and exiting his back under his left shoulder blade.

When Longarm swung his pistol back to his left, the lanky kid was up and running and stumbling off through the brush toward the creek. Arms and legs flopping, he looked like a giant scarecrow blowing away on a cyclone.

"Stop or take it in the back, son!"

The kid bellowed and disappeared, brush thrashing and crackling, and there was a splash as his boots plunged into the stream.

Longarm looked at Jake and then at the other man. They both lay still. Cursing, he stepped over the dead man beside him and strode purposefully toward the stream. The kid gave another bellow as he stumbled up the opposite bank and turned back toward the camp. In the starlight, Longarm could see the large, dark stain on his shirt, beneath his open rat-hair coat. His wet leather chaps glistened.

The kid had a long-barreled Colt in his hand, and as he swung around toward Longarm, he shouted, "You kilt me, you bastard!"

Standing at the lip of the near bank, Longarm extended his Colt straight out from his shoulder. The pistol exploded twice, leaping and flashing. The lanky kid grunted twice, stumbling back before twisting around, sobbing, and dropping to his knees. The kid gave another sob, then fell forward on his face. His spurs flashed in the starlight as his feet spasmed.

Longarm lowered the smoking Colt. He immediately flicked open the loading gate, plucked out the empty shell casings, and filled the chambers with fresh lead. As he walked back over toward the fire, he spun the cylinder, then held the gun low by his side and dropped to a knee beside Jake.

The owlhoot stared straight up at the sky as Longarm

reached into his wool-lined denim coat and pulled a small wad of greenbacks from the man's right front shirt pocket. Longarm spread the bills in his gloved left hand, counting them.

"Fifty dollars," he said, scowling, shaking his head.

He pocketed the Stoneville loot and had just started walking over toward the other man when a rifle cracked upstream. The report echoed shrilly around the canyon. Heavy foot thuds followed, and a man stumbled out of the darkness from a tangle of piñons and junipers. He was an older gent with curly gray hair puffing out around his derby hat. He wore a long black coat and gloves with the fingers cut off. A black, fist-sized hole gaped in his forehead, and blood and white brain matter oozed out over his left eye and cheek. Both eyes rolled back in his head, and he dropped the rifle in his hands before he himself gave a grunt and fell on top of it.

Longarm stood crouching, Colt extended, heart thudding as he looked around skeptically.

"Halloo the camp," a young woman's voice called from the darkness behind the most recently dead man.

"Don't tell me, let me guess," said Longarm dryly. "You're friendly."

Beyond the sphere of flickering firelight, a shadow jostled and then Jenny May walked into the light and stared down at the dead gray-haired man. She wore a long wool coat and a black hat, and she held a Winchester carbine down in her gloved right hand. Gray smoke curled from the barrel. Her tawny hair was pulled back in a ponytail.

Lifting her gaze to Longarm's, she said, "Seen him moving around out here and figured he wasn't up to much good. Guess he was s'posed to bushwhack you while the others kept you distracted."

"Where in the hell did you come from?"

"Nowhere. After I got myself settled down, I decided I'd follow you, show you a shortcut to the May ranch first thing tomorrow."

He glanced at the rifle in her hand and indicated it with his Colt's barrel. "You're the second young lady I've run into today who's right handy with a long gun."

"Make you nervous?"

"You shouldn't be out here."

"If I wasn't, this fella'd be pickin' your pockets about now and drinkin' your coffee." Jenny looked at her Winchester. "A girl growin' up out here has to learn early how to shoot and shoot well if she wants to hold off all the long-coulee riding sons of bitches who haunt these mountains. I can't tell you how many have tried to get me on my back, and not all of 'em cared if I was still breathin' when they did it."

Longarm holstered his pistol, poked his hat brim off his forehead, and jerked his head toward the coffeepot. "Cup o' mud, Miss May?"

Chapter 17

Jenny May led her horse into the camp. She picketed the skewbald paint with the others, then filled the coffeepot at the creek and started a fresh batch brewing on the built-up fire.

Meanwhile, Longarm took from the other two dead men the stolen money Laughing Lyle had paid them to clean him off his backtrail, then dragged their bodies a hundred yards upstream, where he'd leave it up to the coyotes and bobcats to do the final interring. Wasting time on the formal burial of men who'd tried to kill him just wasn't Longarm's style, and he doubted that Billy Vail would fault him for it even if the chief marshal ever found out about it, which wasn't likely.

"It's not that I don't appreciate your help," Longarm told Jenny as he walked back into the camp, "but you shouldn't be out here. I'm here, risking my own life and my horse's, because I have to be."

"Same here." Jenny cracked a branch over her knee

and dropped it onto the fire, on which the coffeepot gurgled and chugged. "I have to help you run my brother down and kill him like the dog he is . . . before he kills Pa, which he'll likely have to do if he tries takin' horses out of our corral."

"He's only allowed back if he's dead. That it?"

"That's right. I should have killed him myself, stopped the whole charade he was puttin' on at Doc Bell's."

"You know it was a charade?"

"Now I do. Don't you?"

Longarm stared down at the fire, thumbs hooked behind his cartridge belt. "Bell knew, didn't he? That's what he was trying to tell me just before he died?"

"That's how I see it."

"Lyle was wounded bad enough to pose no real threat to me, or to ride out of Nowhere right away, but he was pretendin' to be at death's door, and the doctor corroborated his story because Lyle promised him a cut of the money that Bethany hid along the trail somewhere. And who in hell wouldn't believe a doctor . . . especially when he's such a damn good liar?"

Longarm chuckled and ran a gloved hand across his nose. "This morning I saw a breakfast plate beside Lyle's bed. The doc said it was his. But I remember now that I'd seen another plate on Bell's desk when Butter and I first entered the office."

Longarm looked at her squatting there by the coffeepot—a tough, practical girl of unexpected beauty. "Speaking of Butter?" he said, posing it as a question.

Jenny shook her head, then scuttled back against her saddle, stretching out her slender legs clad in patched denims and crossing her stockmen's boots. "I don't know. I reckon he's poor enough, desperate enough, like most everyone else in the town. My brother is an evil man. Most folks around him long, the weakest ones, get tainted by it."

"Like Bethany Todd?"

"Why not?" Jenny shook her hair back. "I seen 'em together before, riding together up here in the mountains. Lyle was good with women. She was likely why he was so intent on getting back to Nowhere. He knew she'd help him."

Longarm arched a skeptical brow. "Just a coincidence she and her father happened to find him along the trail two nights ago?"

Jenny hiked a shoulder. She paused, then changed the subject. "Pa barred him from the ranch when I was old enough to fall under his influence. Oh, he's been back a few times, but mostly he just steals a few horses to supply his gang, laughs in that taunting way of his, and gallops on out. We hear about his depredations when we go to town."

Longarm squatted by the fire. The pot was boiling, so he removed it from the fire with the leather swatch, opened the lid, and tossed in a handful of coffee from his Arbuckles pouch. "The town seems to harbor no ill feelings against you. It's rare for folks not to hold family responsible for their kin's doin's."

"I reckon they know how bad my pa has taken the way Lyle turned out. His only son. So devilish and enjoys bein' devilish, like he tries his best at it. Pa said Lyle's mother was like that—pretty but devilish—and that's where Lyle got it, but Pa's never been nothin' but good and hardworking though he turned to drink because of Lyle and my ma's death."

"Pretty but devilish," Longarm said as the coffee returned to a boil. "That's sort of like Bethany Todd, ain't it?" He couldn't get her off his mind.

Jenny shook her head. "I told you—folks who get under Lyle's influence for whatever reason end up as bad as him."

When Longarm had poured them each a cup of coffee, Jenny said, "Oh, I forgot." She set her cup aside, reached into her saddlebags, and pulled out some blankets and a bottle. "Ma Marcus sent you this. She said it'd keep the chill away."

She handed the bottle over to Longarm, and he grabbed the bottle, chuckling. "Now, that there is a good woman." He held the bottle up to Jenny. "A libation, Miss May? Chilly and gonna get chillier."

"Couldn't stomach the stuff after what I seen it do to Pa."

"Understood." Longarm popped the cork and splashed some of the whiskey into his coffee. Setting the bottle aside, he swirled his coffee around and sipped. He couldn't have asked for a more soothing, delicious brew, except, of course, some of his own Maryland rye.

He glanced at Jenny, who sat with her blankets drawn up to her chin, arms crossed on her chest. She still wore her hat, and her brown eyes reflected the fire's flickering glow. "You worried about your pa?"

She bunched her lips and shook her head. "Not really. Oh, Pa'll take some shots at Lyle if he gets a chance, but Lyle probably already got there by now, stole some horses, and left. Pa probably didn't even stir."

"Lyle won't kill your pa?"

She glanced at Longarm, and there was a dark hesitation in her eyes. Then she returned her gaze to the fire and shook her head once more. "He wouldn't go that far—shoot his feeble old man." She paused. Then she rolled onto her side and curled her legs toward her belly, snuggling in for the night. "Not even Lyle would do somethin' as poison mean as that."

Jenny paused again before adding, "I'll show you a shortcut in the morning. That'll shave an hour off the trip."

"Sounds good, Jenny."

Longarm sipped his coffee and whiskey. It nourished him, warmed him. But he kept his eyes skinned on the darkness beyond the fire, wary of more interlopers, though he doubted there would be anyone else out here this late.

When he finished his coffee, he checked on the horses and took a swing around the camp. He saw nothing but some coyote-sized shadows scurrying around the four dead men in the brush, and he gave a wry, satisfied grunt.

He went back to the fire, kicked out of his boots, and rolled into his blankets. Sometime later, he opened his eyes and lifted his head, holding his breath and looking around. But it was the girl who'd awakened him. The fire had burned down to umber coals, but he could see her to his right rolling around beneath her blankets, groaning and muttering, "Comin', Pa. Lyle's comin' for you!" She sobbed, groaned. "No, Lyle, you bastard . . . don't you dare hurt Pa!"

Longarm saw that her blanket was twisted around

her waist. As she continued to groan and thrash miserably, he rose from his own hotroll, chucked a couple of good-sized branches on the fire to warm the camp a bit, then crabbed over to her. She lay on her back, muttering incoherently now, hair a tangled mass across her tanned cheeks and strong but delicate nose. Her shirt had opened a ways, and he could see the curve of a tender breast lightly sprayed with cinnamon freckles.

Longarm pulled the blanket up to her neck, saying softly, "Shhh, Miss Jenny. Everything's all right." He placed the back of his hand gently against her cheek. "It's just a dream, girl. Just a—"

She sat up with a gasp, hair tumbling around her shoulders.

"Easy," Longarm said. "You were dreaming."

Her breasts and shoulders rose and fell sharply with each labored breath. "Oh," she said finally, thinly. She turned to him, looked into his eyes, her own still bright with fear, and then she gave a sob and threw her arms around his neck. She clung to him tightly, her quick breaths warm and moist against his unshaven neck.

He wrapped his arms around her, splayed his hand across her back, giving her a gentle, reassuring squeeze and trying not to notice the press of her tender mounds against his chest.

"Just a dream," he said.

She drew back away from him and sighed. "Whew!" She smiled and looked around. "I dreamt . . . I dreamt that Lyle was. . . ."

"It was just a dream, Jenny," Longarm said. "You go back to sleep now. You'll feel better once the sun comes up."

She gave a shiver despite the warmth pushing out from the fire's dancing flames. "Cold," she said. "I must've been sweating." She looked up at him from beneath her brows, still quivering. "Would you lay with me for a bit? You're so big and"—he eyes flicked across his chest—"warm."

Longarm hesitated. Of their own accord, his eyes flicked to her heaving bosoms and the spray of freckles in her cleavage. She clutched her arms and gave another shiver.

"Sure," he said. "I'll lay here for a while."

"Thanks, Marshal."

"Friends call me Longarm."

She swallowed and lay back, and when he had dragged his own blankets over and lain down with her, pulling his blankets and hers over them, she buried her head in his chest and said, "All right, then . . . Longarm."

He'd almost managed to fall asleep when he felt her warm hands lightly massaging his iron-hard cock, which was painfully tightening his pants and long handles around his balls. For a moment, he thought she was dreaming, but then her little, warm fingers had unbuttoned his trousers. She slid one of her hands into his pants and through the fly of his balbriggans to cup his balls, gently squeezing.

Her small hand burned against him.

Longarm groaned, blinking up at the stars that he couldn't see for the warm vail of heart-thudding lust that had so suddenly engulfed him. She kept her head pressed against his chest as she delicately hefted his balls and then slowly ran her hand up the throbbing shaft to its head and down again.

She wrapped her hand around it tightly and began pumping. As she pumped him, he could feel her head moving against him, hear her giving little animal grunts and sighs, feel her breasts pressing against him as her breaths grew more and more labored. Christ, Longarm thought, should I say something? Does she know what she's doing or is the poor child asleep?

Then again, he sure as hell didn't want her to stop. She'd seemed so young and virginal, but she was handling his cock like she'd done it before.

He lay back against her saddle, groaning as she manipulated him and made little grunting sounds. At last she stopped, rolled back on her butt, and began furiously opening her pants and then squirming around as she worked them down her legs. Longarm unhitched his own belt and followed suit, grinding his heels into the ground and arching his back while lifting his ass up off the ground far enough to get his whipcord trousers down around his ankles. He'd gotten them only as far as his knees, however, when Jenny swooped over him once more, shoving him back down against the ground and straddling him.

"I've only done this once before," she said in a voice pinched with desperation, "so you tell me if I'm doin' anything, wrong, okay?"

He grunted that he would.

She had her own pants and underwear all the way off, and as she reached down and grabbed him and steadied him, she slowly lowered her pussy over the head of his cock. She squeezed her eyes closed and chomped down on her lower lip. "Shit!" she cried. "It's so damn *big!*"

But then she lowered herself further and fairly screamed. "Oh, *gawd!*" she cried as she clamped her knees tight against him and shivered as though chilled, though Longarm doubted she was cold any longer. Her skin was on fire. Her snatch felt like a pot of warm honey sliding up and down on his tender cock, nerves firing ripples of pure erotic ecstasy up through his belly and heart and into his throat and brain.

As she continued to grunt away on top of him, he opened her shirt and slid it down her shoulders. She kept her eyes closed, oblivious to everything but her snatch, it seemed, as he lifted her thin, cotton chemise above her breasts. He cupped her breasts in his hands, flicked his thumbs across the nipples, then lifted his head and sucked each distended nipple in turn.

"*Ohhhhh!*" she fairly sobbed, bobbing up and down on him faster, with even more desperation. "Ohhhh, *God*, that feels so *good*. Keep doing that, Longarm. I love how your mustache brushes against my tits! God, your tongue is so *hot!*"

No hotter than she was, he thought, tensing himself and squeezing her breasts gently in his hands as he felt her grind against him, shaking like she was lightning-struck as she reached her climax. She opened her mouth to scream, but Longarm closed one hand over her lips and held her down close against him as he bucked up hard against her and let go of his own hot juices, and they lay there, shaking, Jenny continuing to grind his pussy against his spasming organ.

They lay together for a long time, spent. She kept her face pressed against his cheek, occasionally moving her crotch around on his relaxed but still tingling member.

Finally, she sandwiched his face in her hands and whispered, "Did I do it right?"

"You did it just right."

"God, I needed that, Longarm!"

She kissed him passionately, sighed, and rolled off of him, then rose and walked naked to the creek. Her bare ass and legs were pale in the darkness. He drew several deep breaths, then pulled his long handles and trousers back up on his hips and buckled his belt.

When she came back, she dried herself with a scrap of cloth, pulled her pants back on, and lay back down beside him in the bedroll. She pressed her head to his ribs, curling her body into a tight ball against him, and soon her breaths were coming deep and regular.

He woke later when she stirred. He opened his eyes and saw her standing over him with her rifle in her hands. Loudly, she racked a cartridge into the chamber and aimed the rifle at his head.

Chapter 18

Ah, shit—out of the frying pan and into the fire, Longarm thought, staring into the rifle's bottomless black maw.

Blinking sleep from his eyes, he followed the rifle up past its stock and her well-filled work shirt to Jenny's pretty head, which was not canted toward him but facing off toward the north. The sky above the girl was smeared with the pearl wash of dawn. In the faint light, he saw that she was not aiming the rifle at him, as he'd thought upon waking. She was only standing near him and holding it negligently across her hips, though she had the hammer cocked.

Longarm nudged the barrel aside, wagged his head with relief, and said, "What is it?"

"Something thrashing around upstream."

Longarm heard it, too—the snorts and snarls and snapping brush of the predators fighting over Jake and his kith.

"Just coyotes," Longarm said, rising stiffly with a grunt. "They're enjoyin' their breakfast, and I gotta say I'm right jealous. All I have is some jerky tougher than double eagles and some hardtack that redefines 'hard.' "

Jenny depressed the carbine's hammer and leaned the rifle against a tree. "Longarm?" She looked at him shyly, then swept her mess of long, tawny hair back from her shoulders, arranging it into a ponytail. "About last night . . ."

"Ah, hell," Longarm said. "You don't need to go feelin' guilty, and I sure as hell . . ."

"No," she said, lowering her hands and walking toward him, her hair secured with a leather thong behind her head. She placed her hands on his forearms and looked up at him. "Call me wanton or depraved or just a plain old bad girl, but I enjoyed it." A smile lifted her mouth corners. "And I wanted to thank you for it. For taking my mind off Pa and Lyle and all, when there was nothin' for us to do about 'em anyway. Like I said, it was only my second time, and . . . well, I hope you found some pleasure in it, too."

"Jenny?" Longarm said, placing his hands on her arms. "How could I not have?"

He pulled her against him, hugging her, and she wrapped her arms around his waist.

"In that case," she said, pulling away from him and crouching over her saddlebags. "Let's have us some breakfast. Ma packed bacon biscuits and fresh deer jerky. By the time we're finished eating, it should be light enough for us to hit the trail."

"Well, I'll be damned," Longarm said as his stomach rumbled. "That Ma's a caution, ain't she?"

* * *

Jenny had been right. When they'd built up the fire and heated the coffee, with which they washed down Ma Marcus's biscuits and jerky, the sun had risen enough to make travel possible over the rough terrain ahead. When Longarm had turned the mounts of last night's cutthroats' loose, free to stray off to the nearest ranch, Jenny led the way up out of the gorge and back onto the main trail.

A half hour later, they were following the shortcut she'd mentioned. It was a perilously narrow trail along the shoulder of a high mountain on which very little grew except short, brown grass, low-growing evergreen shrubs, and wiry wildflowers. The incline was nearly vertical, and the slope was covered with slide-rock, but the trail, likely carved out of the mountain by deer and elk, was wide enough to give passage, albeit a sometimes harrowing one. He and Jenny were about a thousand feet above a broad mountain park in which a blue lake nestled in a clearing among firs and lodgepole pines.

The rising sun glittered on the water, from which, as Longarm glanced down, a blue heron took ungainly flight and swept off toward the east, toward a pass that stood among steep, toothy peaks.

The trail wound around the mountain, then dropped down into a park not unlike the one on the other side, and Jenny led Longarm onto a rugged two-track trail that branched off away from the mountain and into a broad valley between humpbacked, fir-forested ridges. As they came out of the trees, Longarm saw a small ranch headquarters nestled at the bottom of the valley's right slope,

behind a peeled log portal decorated with elk antlers.
A brand was burned into the portal's overhead timber,
but Longarm couldn't see it yet from his distance of a
hundred yards.

From here, the ranch didn't appear much—just a
small, weathered-gray log cabin and a log barn, flanked
by a privy and fronted by a windmill and three corrals,
including a circular breaking corral. Smoke curled from
the cabin's stone chimney, which climbed up the near
side wall, nearly as broad as the wall itself.

There appeared to be a dozen or so horses inside one
of the corrals, and two figures were moving toward it
from the direction of the cabin. Something was wrong
with one of the figures. The man seemed to be staggering, falling, then heaving himself back to his feet uncertainly.

Angry voices rose on the cool, mid-morning air—
one shriller, more pinched than the other.

"Oh, no," Jenny said softly as, holding her reins up
high against her chest, she stared straight ahead toward
the ranch.

The pinched voice rose again, more clearly now:
*"No, you don't, damn your worthless hide! I don't care
if you are kin of mine—you ain't takin' no more of my
hosses, you gutless, low-down dirty dog!"*

The stumbling figure now lurched up off a knee and
dove toward the other man, who was in front of him and
striding slowly, arrogantly toward the corral with the
horses in it. As Longarm and Jenny continued riding, the
headquarters growing larger before them, Longarm saw
Laughing Lyle's pinto vest and the long, stringy, straw-

colored hair hanging straight down from his flat-brimmed hat.

Behind the men, another figure, who wore brown pants and a black vest, stood in the yard before the cabin, facing them, one foot cocked forward, a hand on a hip, taking in the skirmish with a casual, jeering air. Longarm recognized the supple, long-legged figure of Bethany Todd. She appeared to be holding a mug in her hand. Behind her, the cabin's front door was open.

"Pa, no!" Jenny screamed as Laughing Lyle spun suddenly and hammered the older man's face with his right fist.

Longarm could hear the smack of the killer's fist against his father's face even as Jenny ground her spurs into her horse's flanks and set off at a gallop.

"Jenny, goddamnit, hold on!" Longarm yelled, reaching forward to slide his Winchester from his saddle boot.

He rammed his heels against his buckskin's loins and lunged on up the trail behind Jenny, seeing her father hit the ground hard with a loud yell as Laughing Lyle swung back to face the oncoming riders. Lyle clawed one of his two six-shooters from its holster, strode forward several steps, and raised the pistol straight out from his right arm.

"Jenny!" Longarm shouted, cocking his rifle one-handed. "Get your damn head down!"

The girl kept barreling straight ahead, hunkered low over her horse's neck but not low enough to keep from getting herself drilled if Laughing Lyle's aim was keen, and if he'd actually sling lead at his own half-sister.

Longarm wasn't all that surprised when, a half a second after Laughing Lyle's pistol puffed smoke from its barrel, dust blew up only two feet away from Jenny's lunging sorrel mare.

Too close to be merely trying to scare her off.

Longarm urged more speed from the buckskin and began to overtake Jenny's sorrel as he aimed his Winchester one-handed and squeezed the trigger. The rifle shrieked, but the bullet was thrown wide by the shooter's jostling perch, and dust puffed a good six feet to Laughing Lyle's right, near the base of the breaking corral's gatepost.

"Jenny, get back," Longarm shouted again, galloping five feet behind her as she tore under the portal and into the ranch yard.

Longarm galloped into the yard behind her, just as Laughing Lyle's pistol smoked once more. Jenny gave a shriek and went tumbling off her sorrel's left hip, hitting the ground in a thudding pile only a few feet from Longarm's buckskin. Longarm levered another shell one-handed into the Winchester's breech, aimed the same way as before, and fired as he continued lunging toward Laughing Lyle, who'd turned his pistol on Longarm.

The lawman's next shot must have creased him, because the killer's own shot spanged off a rock far wide of its fast-closing target, and then he yowled and spun around, grabbing his ear. Longarm barreled toward the man, triggering the Winchester twice more before Laughing Lyle snapped a shot at his father and took off running toward the cabin.

Bethany stood in the doorway, pumping a Winchester. One shot blew the lawman's hat off his head a half second before the next one punched into the buck-skin's brisket.

The horse screamed and dropped its head and withers.

"Shit!" the lawman cried, throwing his rifle wide and then flinging himself free of the saddle.

The heart-shot horse turned a complete somersault before landing with a crunching thud in the yard, mak-ing dust roil about ten feet from where Hy May sat up on one hip, clutching his other knee with one hand and shouting, "*Jen-neeee!*"

Three more slugs triggered from the cabin's doorway blew up dirt and ground horse shit in front of Longarm as he rolled onto his belly and brought up his Colt. He triggered three quick shots toward the cabin, blowing slivers from the casing and evoking a clipped shriek from Bethany, who lowered her carbine and ducked inside just as Laughing Lyle dove past her into the cabin.

Longarm fired two more shots, but they only hit more wood as Bethany kicked the door closed. He could hear them both yelling inside as he glanced at the old man now calling for Jenny and crying as he lay on his side, legs curled beneath him. He'd obviously been badly beaten, for both eyes were swollen nearly shut and there were deep bruises and cuts on his patch-bearded face.

"Gotta get you to cover," Longarm told the old man as he quickly hooked his arms under May's. The old rancher wore a ratty undershirt and patched canvas trou-sers and suspenders, and he smelled like old sweat and an entire vat of forty-rod. His hair was long and greasy, and it clung to his withered yet not unhandsome face.

"He's a devil, that one," Hy May said in a gravelly

voice thick from drink. "Pure-dee evil. Came here last night, beat hell out of me with a chunk of cordwood while that girl used my possibles to cook 'em supper. Left me piled up in my own livin' room, detailin' all the torment they've inflicted!"

May cursed his son roundly.

"Go to Jenny! Go to my daughter!" he sobbed as Longarm dragged him around behind the nearest corral.

"Sit tight," Longarm told him, as he ran back out from behind the corral, toward where Jenny lay on her side on the ground where her half-brother's shots had deposited her.

Longarm was halfway to Jenny, flicking glances back toward the cabin, knowing that its two devilish occupants would be throwing lead at him soon, when they did just that, two rifles cracking, the slugs hammering the ground just behind Longarm's thudding heels.

"Hey, Longarm!" Laughing Lyle shouted from the window. "How'd you like my little ruse in town, lawdog?" He laughed raucously, jeeringly. "Not a bad way to hole up for a time and heal from them pills you gave me back at Finlay's, eh?"

Another bullet spanged off a near rock as Longarm crouched over Bethany. He raised his rifle and snapped off three shots toward the cabin, watching splinters fly from the casings of the two windows in which he'd glimpsed the faces of both Laughing Lyle and the preacher's daughter. Inside, Laughing Lyle laughed wildly, tauntingly, as Longarm set his rifle down, grabbed one of Jenny's arms, and pulled her up and over his left shoulder.

She groaned and shook her head. Blood spotted her temple where her half-brother's bullet had creased her.

Longarm adjusted the girl on his shoulder, then grabbed his rifle. Bullets began flying once more from the cabin, puffing dust around him, screeching off rocks. As he ran as fast as he could toward a shallow wash about seventy yards from the cabin and straight across from the corrals, one of the bullets burned across his right thigh.

He growled deep in his chest, flaring his nostrils. His brown eyes were hard as granite.

The burn in his leg stoked the already blazing fires of rage in his belly to a white-hot conflagration.

He dashed down into the wash, and as several more slugs kicked up dirt from the lip of its bank, he lowered Jenny to the gravelly ground.

"What you gonna do now, Longarm?" Laughing Lyle shouted, laughing, from the cabin. "We're in here, with plenty of ammo, and you're out there with likely damn little by now!"

Bethany's voice yelled, "Best call it quits, lawman. Best go on back to town and lick your wounds. Me an' my man are gonna take that Stoneville loot, grab us some horses from the corral yonder, and head for Mexico. *And there ain't one blasted thing you can do about it!*"

They both laughed raucously—human jackals kicking up dust at some unholy fandango thrown by the devil himself.

Longarm grabbed his rifle and punched fresh lead through the loading gate. He shouldered up against the wash's bank and edged a look over the lip toward the cabin.

"That's where you're wrong," he said, punching the ninth cartridge into the rifle's receiver, then levering a round into the chamber. "I'll tell you two sons o' rotten, bitter bitches what I'm gonna do about it. I'm going to kill you both!"

"What's that, Longarm?" Lyle called.

"I said you'd best say your prayers, Lyle. Bethany, I'm talkin' to you, too!" Longarm climbed to his feet. "Say 'em now, 'cause you both got about one more minute to live!"

He fairly hurled himself up and over the bank and set off running toward the cabin, snarling like a rogue griz with fresh meat on the wind.

Chapter 19

As smoke puffed from windows on either side of the cabin's closed front door, Longarm sprinted, bobbing and weaving, before he stopped suddenly and fired his Winchester. His bullet sailed through the window right of the door, evoking a howl from Bethany, who pulled her head back in as her hat tumbled off her shoulder.

Longarm took off running, bobbing, and weaving once more, Laughing Lyle's bullets screeching around him, blowing up sage shrubs and rocks, one slicing a hot line across the lawman's neck just below his left ear.

Again, Longarm stopped, aimed quickly, and fired. His bullet crashed against Laughing Lyle's rifle barrel, and the killer screeched and dropped the rifle out the window. It clattered into the yard at the base of the cabin. Longarm ejected the spent cartridge and fired three more times, lifting a staccato rhythm, the shots echoing around the ridges. He heard his first shot hit something soft and fleshy, evoking a hoarse scream and a bellowing curse.

"Lyle!" cried Bethany, her voice muffled.

Longarm ran straight toward the cabin, quickly punching fresh ammo through the smoking Winchester's loading gate. The door was constructed of what appeared to be halved log timbers, too stout to bust through without a battering ram, so Longarm headed for Bethany's window, to the door's right.

He racked a fresh round into the Winchester's chamber and stretched his strides, snarling and growling through gritted teeth as he ran, pumping his arms and legs, remembering the dead people in Stoneville, his friend Case Morgan, and Preacher Todd—not to mention the multiple ruses Laughing Lyle and Bethany had pulled on Longarm himself.

When he was five feet from the window—there was no glass in it and the shutter was open—he lofted himself into the air. He dove straight on through and into the cabin, twisting his airborne body in the air and firing the Winchester twice toward his left a half-second before he hit the floor with a loud grunt. He caught a glimpse of two shadowy figures on that side of the cabin, the blond-headed one scrambling back into the cabin's depths, screaming, while Laughing Lyle fell back against the far wall. His blood pumped from a shoulder wound, and there was a bloody line across his left cheek just beneath his eye. His previous wounds had also opened up, and all the blood had turned his hickory shirt bright red.

He had a pistol in each hand, and he threw his head back, laughing, as he raised both six-shooters toward Longarm, who, propped on a hip, fired the Winchester, quickly jacking the cocking lever. All three slugs hammered Laughing Lyle's chest, one after another, making him jerk as though struck by lightning, as he triggered his pistols into the floor around his feet.

He was still laughing bizzarely as he continued to trigger the pistols, while trying to raise them, though they appeared to have become chunks of lead in his hands. A gun blasted to Longarm's right, shattering a lantern on a low table beside a rocking chair.

Longarm swung around to see Bethany stumbling back against a rear door in the kitchen portion of the cabin, triggering a pistol toward Longarm, who fired twice and then watched as the girl got the door open and stumbled through it and into the cabin's backyard.

Longarm gained his feet quickly, wincing at the throbbing pain in his shoulder that had hit the floor hard, and turned to Laughing Lyle, who knelt in front of the window on the far side of the cabin, laughing hysterically, mouth forming a horseshoe, eyes brightly insane. He held both pistols straight down by his sides. Both blasted loudly into the floor, then dropped from his hands.

Blood ran down his ugly face and pumped from the fresh holes in his chest.

Suddenly, he quit laughing and stared at Longarm blankly, pain and horror gradually leeching into his gaze.

"Ah, shit," he said.

He fell forward. With a solid thud he hit the floor, padded with a faded, blood-splattered burgundy rug. Laughing Lyle jerked a few times and lay still.

Longarm swung around and headed for the half-open back door, catching a glimpse of the saddlebags he'd been seeking slung over a cracked leather sofa, several piles of greenbacks sitting neatly on one of the stuffed cushions. Apparently, Laughing Lyle and Bethany had been counting the loot earlier, while Mr. May groaned in misery, watching them helplessly, most likely.

Longarm strode past the couch and out the back door. Beyond, he could see Bethany staggering away from the cabin through the brush and stunt cedars. Longarm walked out along the well-worn path that led to the privy and continued on past it through a ragged stand of pines and junipers.

When he'd pushed through the brush, he saw Bethany about twenty yards ahead, staggering across a narrow, shallow stream that ran along the base of the forested northern ridge. She swung around uncertainly. Blood spotted her right side. It smeared her forehead. Her teeth were a white line between drawn back lips, and her green eyes were hard and cougar-mean.

"Drop it, Bethany," Longarm said, holding his rifle barrel-down at his side.

"You ruined everything!" she screamed. "Lyle and I were going to be rich! What's more—we were gonna be out of *Nowhere!*"

She raised her pistol. Longarm got his Winchester leveled first. It leaped and roared. The bullet took her in the dead center of her chest, between the comely lumps of her breasts. She gave a gasp as it lifted her up and hurled her back until she hit the water with a thump and a splash.

Blood pumped from her chest to soak her shirt and show inky red in the water. Her blond hair floated around her. A crow cawed raucously in the thick forest climbing the ridge beyond her. Longarm thought it sounded like a demon calling the girl back to hell. Along with Laughing Lyle, most likely.

Longarm turned around and walked wearily back toward the cabin. He emerged from the fragrant brush and stopped, tensing.

Town Marshal Roscoe Butter stood before him, holding a cocked Remington revolver. The gun was aimed at Longarm's brisket. Butter looked hard but uncertain. He had the saddlebags of Stoneville loot draped over his left shoulder.

He didn't say anything. He just stared at Longarm. The Remington shook ever-so-slightly in his fist, his knuckles showing white.

"Fancy seein' you out here, Roscoe."

"Shut up, Longarm. This ain't easy for me."

"Nah, I s'pose not. The ruse in town must have been pretty damn hard, too."

"It was!" The Nowhere town marshal glanced past Longarm toward where Bethany lay dead in the stream. "I didn't know about her, though. I didn't know him and her was playin' a double-cross, the bastard."

Longarm smiled mildly. "What'd he do? Promise if you and the doc went along with his play-acting, pretending his wounds were about to kill him, he'd share the loot with you?"

Butter raised the pistol higher. His craggy cheeks flushed. "I told you to shut up, Longarm, or I'll shoot you right now!"

"Well, it looks like you're gonna shoot me, anyway. Might as well let me go to my grave with the satisfaction of knowin' how it was all cut up. I suppose it was you who put the wolfer Dave Ross on my trail—the one whose wick I snuffed in the Nowhere Saloon? He was gonna get a cut, too, I take it?"

Butter shook his head slightly and narrowed an eye as he stared down the barrel of the quivering Remy. "I'm sorry, Longarm. A coupla years ago, I never woulda considered fallin' in with such a scheme. Aligning myself with the likes of Laughin' Lyle. Bell wouldn't have done it, either. But, goddamnit, the railroad abandoned us, and that damn town is dyin', and we got desperate. I got two women and a kid to raise, goddamnit, Longarm!"

"There's plenty of men in worse positions than you, Butter. You have no reason to squawl. You have even less reason to do what you've done and what you're about to do. You ever hear of *honor* and *dignity?*"

The Nowhere marshal flinched as though slapped. Then he bunched his lips angrily. His brown eyes glowed yellow in the midday sunlight. "Turn around. I'll make it quick. You won't know what hit you."

"Forget it," Longarm said, broadening his smile. "You're gonna have to shoot me right here." He tapped his chest.

A familiar voice sounded from the right. "D-drop it, Marshal."

Both Longarm and Butter turned to see Benji Vickers step out from behind the privy. He was aiming a Spencer rifle at Butter. Longarm recognized it as Butter's own carbine.

"Benji, goddamnit," the town marshal barked, "I told you to stay in town!"

Benji shifted his feet, squared his heavy sloping shoulders, and licked his lips. "I c-can't let you do it,

Marshal. It ain't right, what you and Doc Bell did. I never thought it was right. And I ain't gonna let you kill Marshal Long."

He worked his throat, sniffed, and licked his lips again. "Now, you drop that pistol an' them saddlebags. You don't . . ." He squinted down the Spencer's barrel as he drew the heavy hammer back. "I'll shoot you. Sure as you're standin' there with all that money that don't belong to you."

Butter said tightly, "Benji, as your employer, I'm ordering you to drop that rifle, now!"

"Nope. I won't. I appreciate what you done for me, givin' me the badge an' all. But you never thought much of me; you thought I was too stupid to carry a gun, but I'm here to show you that you made a mistake. With your own gun, Marshal. Now, you drop that pistol or I'll shoot you with this rifle, Marshal."

"You don't even know how to shoot that thing."

Benji quirked his lips in a faint, knowing smile but said nothing more.

Longarm lurched forward, swinging his Winchester's rear stock up. It smacked against Butter's hand. His Remington discharged with a loud crack and went sailing out of his grip.

"Ach!" the town marshal cried, buckling to his knees and grabbing his injured hand, eyes spitting sparks at Longarm.

Longarm smashed his right fist against Butter's right jaw. A second later, Butter was flat on his back on the well-tramped privy path. His chest and potbelly rose and fell sharply as he breathed, half-sobbing and half-cursing.

Longarm stared down at him as Benji lowered the rifle and walked slowly over. "Damn, I just didn't take you for that big a fool, Roscoe." Longarm reached down, removed the town marshal's badge from the man's grubby wool vest, and gave it to Benji.

"Here you go, Marshal," he told the big man. "Best haul your prisoner back to town."

Benji switched his uncertain gaze from the badge to Longarm. His lower jaw fell in shock, but his eyes spoke, pleased. Longarm reached down and picked up the saddlebags. He glanced at the bullet burn across his thigh. It wasn't much. He'd tend it with the sundry other ones later.

He slung the saddlebags over his left shoulder and then headed back through the cabin, past the dead and still-staring Laughing Lyle, who did not look like he had much laughter left in him, and out the front door.

Jenny was helping her father toward the cabin, both of them arm-in-arm and walking along the near corral. They were speaking to each other in low, reassuring tones.

"You two all right?" Longarm asked.

They stopped, stared at the tall federal lawman.

Hy May narrowed his eyes angrily. "That devil-spawn of mine dead?"   .

"He is."

"Then we're just fine." May glanced at his daughter. "Come on, girl, let's get us inside. Me? I could use a drink!"

Jenny kept her eyes on Longarm until she'd helped her father through the door and into the cabin. Longarm adjusted the heavy saddlebags on his shoulder and dug a half-smoked cheroot from his coat pocket. He fired the cigar and puffed until he had a good smoke going.

He gave another sigh and leaned his head back against the cabin wall, smoking. Thinking back through it all, he chuckled darkly and shook his head, blowing smoke into the sunny mountain air.

Watch for

**LONGARM AND
THE BANKER'S DAUGHTER**

the 409th novel in the exciting LONGARM
series from Jove

Coming in December!

And don't miss

**LONGARM DOUBLE #4:
LEGEND WITH A SIX-GUN**

Longarm Double Edition

Available from Jove in December!

LONGARM

GIANT-SIZED ADVENTURE FROM AVENGING ANGEL LONGARM.

BY TABOR EVANS

2006 Giant Edition:

LONGARM AND THE
OUTLAW EMPRESS

2007 Giant Edition:

LONGARM AND
THE GOLDEN EAGLE
SHOOT-OUT

2008 Giant Edition:

LONGARM AND THE
VALLEY OF SKULLS

2009 Giant Edition:

LONGARM AND THE
LONE STAR TRACKDOWN

2010 Giant Edition:

LONGARM AND THE
RAILROAD WAR

penguin.com/actionwesterns

M456AS0510